The Adventures of Tom McGuire

The Dream Catcher

BY RAYNER TAPIA

9/5/14

The Adventures of Tom McGuire

The Dream Catcher

Enjoy the adventure
Milo

Copyright © 2011 Rayner Tapia
All rights reserved.

ISBN: 1466353775
ISBN 13: 9781466353770

Other Titles in the Series:

The Adventures of Tom McGuire©

The Bard of Typhoeusina©

Morkann's Revenge©

The Dream Catcher©

The Curse of King Cepheus - A Broken Enchantment©

Morkann's Nemesis©

By Rayner Tapia

Visit the website for more information:
www.theadventuresoftommcguire.com©

Quotes from some of my favourite laureates:

*'Logic will get you from A to B.
Imagination will get you everywhere.'*
Albert Einstein

*'The difficulty of literature is not to write,
but to write what you mean.'*
Robert Louis Stevenson

In Loving Memory of My Dad

Acknowledgements

Thank you to my wonderful family and some special key people in my life:

Joy, Amber, Karen, Michelle, Meriyem, Astrid, Diya, and all of my friends who never gave up on me
—Thank you, my angels

and

George Ruddock — for all your support

To my Mum for everything you do!

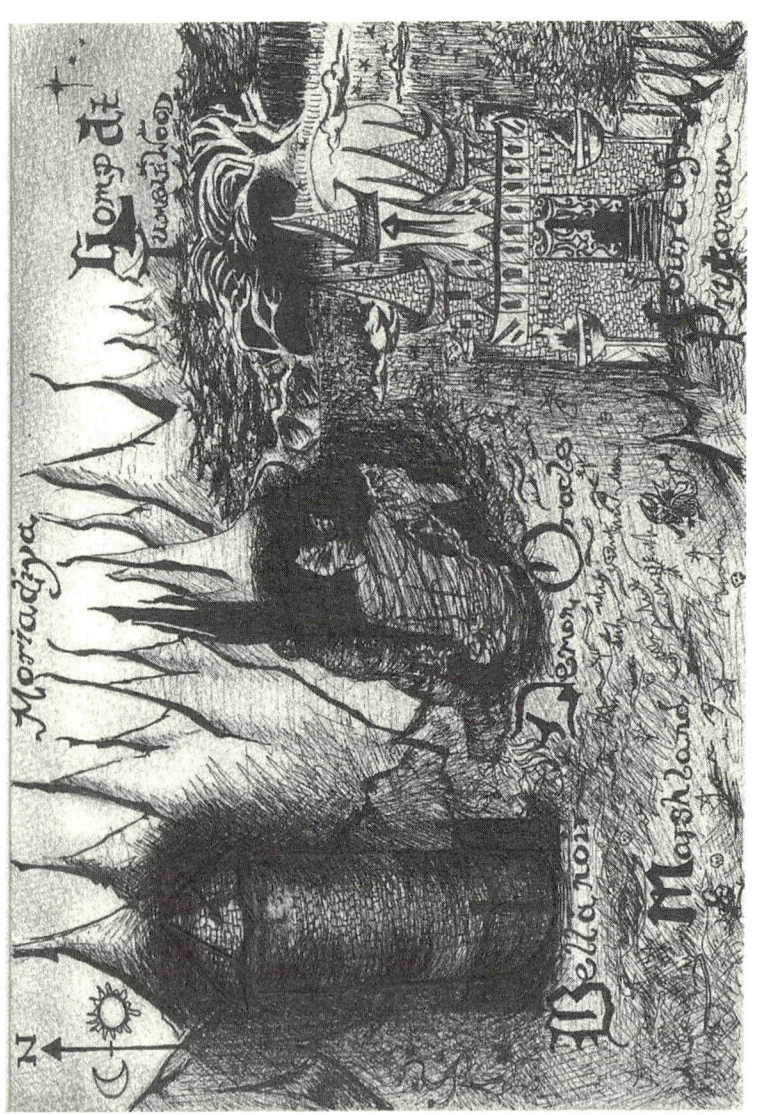

Table of Contents

Chapter I
Hayley's Star · 1

Chapter II
The Hoop with Feathers · 19

Chapter III
The Valley of Tongues ·41

Chapter IV
The Calm beneath the Surface · 71

Chapter V
Carina's Drift · 83

Chapter VI
Beneath the Calm ·95

Chapter VII
The Lost Princess · 99

Chapter 1

This Chapter contains Latin

Hayley's Star

That morning all seemed calm. James was all tucked up in his bed safe and sound; he glared up at the ceiling. He could hear nothing apart from the sound of the curtains blowing in the breeze from the slightly opened window. He contemplated the week's events and what had happened. He pondered to himself as the sun's rays danced on his eyelids.

He breathed silently and whispered to himself, 'I always knew there was something strange about that teacher!' He thought about Mrs. Morecraft's actions and how she would snarl at him whenever he walked past her. He would just look down, not understanding why she did this. He thought about how Tom would constantly tell him of his distrust and dislike of Mrs. Morecraft and how she would always try and make his life difficult.

It had been an extraordinary series of events and an adventurous week, but strangely enough this day felt just like any other day; there was a sense of normality in the air. The sky was blue and crisp with only the muted buzzing sounds of the street cars zooming through the roads.

The Dream Catcher

James became distressed. He glared down at the floor, sad and lonely he was feeling aloof. He was reminiscing about his true friendships he had made, about the princess and the strange girl with hooves, Halaconia, whom he found captivating. He contemplated how he thought he would just leave Tom in the strange wilderness alone. James became angry with himself for thinking such a thing.

'Gosh to think I would have done that!' Frowning, he pondered in deep thought reflecting back to when Morkann had grappled with his mother who had swiped him off from the floor like some celestial creature.

This, of course, was the first time he had witnessed that his mother, Linda, had any powers beyond his wildest dreams. He could never have imagined seeing his mother in her divine form.

However, he realised that his mother was very special. He began to comprehend why she was so protective—that she was a life form from a world where beings and creatures survived only in storybooks. James pondered how she had survived on earth, and he started to imagine what her life must have been like prior to her being on earth.

'I mean she cleans our socks and makes my bed and stuff…' James muttered to himself. He felt very disillusioned and extremely anxious as to how he would approach his mum.

He wondered how he would go about probing her about her past and asking for the answers he so longed to hear. He licked his lips and screwed up his eyes and tried to understand and make sense of the fact that perhaps she too was from the world that he had now seen for himself.

James began to visualize his Mum as an alien! But she couldn't be. She had nothing unusual about her person. The problem was even more irritating that to him she was just Mum. James held

out his arms and stared right through them turning them upside down looking for anything abnormal, mumbling to himself in bewilderment. He wasn't really sure what it was that he was searching for; just looking for anything that would make him try and understand that perhaps he was becoming more accepting of her being from a different planet.

James then reminisced about the first time he'd seen the fragile princess and the wild but beautiful Halaconia, of how her burnished silky hair fell to one side, hiding the flowers covering that one side of her face drooping down to her svelte neck. He also remembered the silver wings, which she used to glide into the galactic airspace with ease. James smiled to himself and remembered it all.

'Wow!' He shook his head in amazement, gulping in a deep breath of air. He then smiled to himself thinking of the princess and of her beauty; yet she was so timid and weak. He remembered how he had first discovered the princess and of her piercing voice, her angelic voice. How she sang such high-pitched notes that the tower crumbled like powder right before his eyes all because of her high notes which perforated even the skies, sending the shooting stars into a firework display.

How her sharp voice tore with a reverberated raze through the Tower of Bellè a Noir, forming broken steps out of the old crumbling tower. The sun beamed onto James's face, forcing him to close his eyes tight as the sun danced on his eyelids, creating a sharp shadow profile on the wall. The princess with her burnished bronze-hair and dewy, sand coloured skin together with her gazelle-shaped eyes and her magnificent voice that sliced the atmosphere was all James could see in his mind.

James was in a lost daze, daydreaming. Still in deep thought, he reminisced about the strange creatures he had met. Halaconia,

The Dream Catcher

who was so beautiful, petite, and with flowers growing along her face and neck with her peculiar hoofed feet and her strange strong silver transparent wings together with luscious, silky, wavy, ebony hair drooping to one side.

At that point James jolted and sat up out of his bed and tried to focus as he stretched out his arms as if trying to pray to the Gods up above. Rolling his eyes in bewilderment, he pondered to himself about the princess who seemed to have taken hold of his thoughts. Where did she go? Who was she? He was baffled; he shook his weary head trying to make sense of the previous day's events.

He threw back the covers from his bed and jolted straight out trying to focus his eyes and awake from his slumber. He rubbed his eyes and glared out of the window and straight to the beam of light luring him in. He stood upright and composed in his red, spotty, cotton pyjama trousers and red, plain t-shirt and gazed, almost hypnotized, straight out of his window. There was nothing to see except for the extremely tall overpowering tree, which he could not recall ever being there. The entire area and tree leaves were sparkling like emeralds and glistening in the morning sun's rays; a bright white light beamed down, as if angles were dancing. James began to become aware of the tall tree, which he had never seen before or had even noticed.

As he stared hard into the tree, his eyes starting to dry out of any moisture, they became sore and red. The more he stared, the more he became hypnotised. His eyes were now frozen open so that the more he gazed the more he could see the mirage of a tree, which seemed to mirror a tall muscular figure, but he was unable to completely determine who the figure was or could be—or indeed was it a figure? Was he seeing things? James desperately shook his head in disbelief.

Hayley's Star

Again, James looked on intently until he was totally transfixed staring directly into space. 'James, where are you going?' shouted Linda again glancing into his face realising he was locked into a magnetic spell. However, James was unable to hear anything, just an incoherent noise. He continued to pace robotically into the yard. James was not sure of the tree, but he was now able to identify branches moving like large arms adorned in verdant greenery to hide the movement as if an anaconda snake were stretching; the enormous muscular body coiled and caught the shimmering of sunlight and then reflected each muscle as a scale in a Gregorian monk's sleeve. The emerald green leaves stretched out and wriggled, moving like fingers to raise and rally together beckoning him to come closer.

James was now completely transfixed, mesmerised by a mirage or an image which seemed to lock him into the gaze of the tree. Something or someone was luring him in; James was unable to control his sense of security.

He knew that he would have to visit the galaxy once more just to discover the origin of the dusky girl he had rescued from the Tower of Belle Noir. It was now apparent that for some strange reason this tree, which seemed to have appeared over night, had something to do with the thought of revisiting the land he had seen only once. The tree seemed to come alive and appeared to be dragging James into its path with its menacing light. As James's gaze became stronger, he seemed now to be possessed. James was totally engrossed; he was glaring into a tree or was it a tree? He was completely gripped in a magnetic sleep. The tree was shining a beam of bright, sharp light. James tried to stare back hoping to see something from his gaze, but the more he concentrated the more he seemed to be fighting a losing battle.

The Dream Catcher

Whatever it was it was something he had no control over. James viewed a small, purple, flickering flame firing back into his gaze. He stared completely and was totally spellbound by the light source sparkling, as it were beckoning him. What could it be that was drawing him closer? Although transfixed by this strange, illuminating light source he was able to wonder about his surroundings. He had lost all control of his self-being and power. He could feel the intensity of the trance; he was able to sense a hypnotic spell. James leant forward and placed one foot in front of the other, and then he dipped his back lunging forward so that he was able to peer outside the window to get a closer look at the tree.

There, he could see it. It was clear, a bright purple, amethyst, warm, illuminating light reflecting a bright sharp prism, inviting him to enter. It was Haley's Star, the star of all lost dreams; it was a light, the flame of hope of Lost Dreams. It was beaming down from the universe through Hakeem who appeared in the image of a colossal tree, a 'Redwood,' nature's wonder; and although huge its branches appeared to disappear into the sun's rays with the image of a branch of a tree hiding its true form with thickly scented spruce branches clutching at his clothes, seeming to slap against his chest and shredding his hand to disappear into the verdant foliage.

The spectrum of light shone brightly, and it was dazzling like a celestial spectrum on a mission. It was beckoning James into the tree.

The sun's rays danced through the green radiant leaves, mixing with the auburn-burnished, brazen bracken of the season's lustre. The rays dazzled on the branches and twinkled on the lichen as if silver dust had been sprinkled across the old, rustic, brown brushwood.

Hayley's Star

James robotically walked out of his bedroom into the landing space quickly dragging his jacket from the peg; he ran down the stairs, brushing past some pictures hanging in the hallway. He didn't turn to see what he was doing—he was totally hypnotized by the beam of bright white light which shone intently.

When he reached the bottom of the stairs he took in a deep breath and pulled his red spot pyjama top straight over his body and hurriedly slid on his thin jacket as if he were a solider marching into battle!

The Kitchen wooden door shot open and Linda, walked towards her son, 'James where are you going?' she asked seeing her son locked in a trance, staggering towards the front door. There was no answer, she tried to grab his arm, to stop him but she had to let go. He slid past her hand, slowly. It was as if he had walked through her body just to get to the light shining through.

'Oh My, Linda watched on helplessly. knowing where he was going and she knew too, that because of King Cepheus, her father, she would not be able to pursue him any further inorder to stop him.

'Tom…Tom' she shouted at the bottom of the stairs calling for him to help his older brother.

He began to slowly pace towards the towering tree, straightening his jacket so as not to feel the brisk cold breeze. James tried to correct his vision by blinking several times. He took small steps in his stride as his heart began to race. James knew something was different. He was curious and his inquisitive mind carried him forward further; however, James felt he was unable to do anything rational

The flickering flame had led James through the dense terrain and had created a path to guide him towards the tree. James had almost reached the tree when he noticed a strange-looking object

The Dream Catcher

hanging from a thin branch. It was a willow's hoop which had white and black, strange, soft, fluffy feathers, horsehair, and small wooden beads with strange offerings on it. James could see that a large black spider had begun to spin a web around the hoop. The spider's silver web had been spun in a pentagon shape so as not to cover the strange coloured beads and horsehair. The whole hoop and where it was hanging seemed rather peculiar.

The hoop looked very bizarre. He was perplexed as to why he had not ever seen this before as it was the weirdest thing he had observed but nonetheless interesting. James took hold of the hoop peering at it from every angle, trying to understand its complexity. He was totally transfixed and frowned, grimacing at the strange object. He held the hoop carefully and then placed it in his jacket pocket. The light source became stronger.

James looked up into the direction of the light source. He was baffled yet he had no control. He then continued to follow the light still looking for an answer and still looking down at his hoop, which now seemed to be lifting in his hand, with each bead dazzling. James knew that the hoop had some power, but what it was he was unsure. He glared intently towards the light still holding the hoop with beads tightly.

He could make out a thick monstrous branch hiding a dark, strong, and powerful muscular arm. The closer he got to the huge object he could see it emerging in the clearing, and it was colossal. The brown, twisted trunk fell over the pavement engulfing the large, rustic, obtruding, spirally areas of the enormous trunk with its old wiry mangled bark which sat on the ground like a heap of old, crumpled, animated wood. The base of the tree was old and wrinkly, appearing dank and very strained with its macabre, gruesome bark growling where it stood proud. James felt drawn towards the obscure tree, the light source was strong, and now this spider's silver web, which had he seen earlier with the strange hoop and horsehair together with odd beads, sparkled, enticing him to walk further deeper in to the terrain. The branch which had led James became closer and nearer, and as the light source became brighter and more intense the tree towered over the entire small surrounding.

James was now totally unaware of where he was going and understanding only that the branches had been used to beckon him to keep moving and walk on. The tree was an old, tall Redwood coast tree with its twisted old macabre branches stretching over the concrete pavement like yesterday's spaghetti, crawling through the ground like worms.

James had never noticed the old tree prior to the morning's events. Therefore he became very bemused and contemplated when and if the tree had just appeared or whether it had been there before. As he was questioning himself he continued to walk on, mesmerised in a trance following the flickering of a dazzling purple light.

'This tree…? Has this always been here?' he whispered to himself.

He precariously and slowly stepped towards the towering monstrous tree. The autumn leaves shimmered in the sunlight, beckoning him, dancing to a gentle breeze, but there was no wind, just a cold shallow chill of a moving shadow hiding in the tree. The towering figure continued to hold out his hand which was a branch engulfed with green foliage covering a thick heavy strong hand. James looked on intently. He was now able to see a muscular dark hand, strong and powerful, directing a sharp light source towards James.

The Dream Catcher

The spectrum of light flickered and created shadows on the pitted concrete ground below. The light created strange obscure shapes of one-eyed, demon monsters with no arms, all of which were engulfing the ground with a thick moss-like substance forming colossal arms that were now swaying with the large shadow.

However, there were no monsters, only these abhorrent shadows dripping within the leaves forming strange wild shapes on the wall. As the Redwood Coast tree appeared nearer, the leaves seemed to twitter and chatter amongst themselves.

The branches were all heavy, old, twisted, and somewhat malevolent, deprived of any life. They were draped in moss and brown, old, silky, wet lichen, and appeared to be gripping onto life as if a giant spider had spun its web over the trunk trying to swallow up the whole tree—immersing itself like a slippery snake which had slithered across its domain or perhaps like quick sand had split into a metropolis.

James staggered on slowly, pacing himself; he was lost in thought and suddenly he hesitated as he approached the towering tree that was now beaming a bright prism of reflective light that had drawn him in so close.

It was reflecting sharply back onto his face, warming his face like a furnace. James raised his arms trying to cover his face, turning his hands in to protect his eyes from the bright beam. He squinted as the light shone down and intensified. He cautiously crept towards the small autumn patch where the unusual Redwood Coast tree stood proud. This was Hakeem.

James was baffled by the tree, which he had never seen before. He cautiously lent forward; he glared as hard as he could. As he gazed deeper and deeper he was able to view not a tree but an extremely

Hayley's Star

tall, overpowering, faceless being draped in what appeared to be a thick heavy cloak, form the trunk of a tree-like shape.

Tom, by this time, had rushed into James's bedroom having heard some noises that had made him startle. He was curious and anxious at James's disappearance. Tom looked on in bewilderment as he watched in fear from the window, at the same time quaking in fear. He licked his lips and frowned, wondering how he should now stop his brother.

He took a fleeting glance around the room then turned to the window which was half open; he peered outside and could see James seeming to walk towards the tree in what appeared to be in a hypnotic trance.

Tom gazed hard and glimpsed back quickly at James as the bright light seemed bewitching and enticed him to tread further. In what felt like seconds Tom quickly rushed to his room and pulled the magic powder and sword that he had from under his bed. Then just like lightening Tom knew he had to rush in to stop James marching into what looked like an abyss, a chasm hiding within the tree. Tom stood quivering with fear, not knowing if Morkann had returned with her army of Ghouls and was waiting for James or even him!

James's life was now in danger, and Tom could sense it. Fearing the worst he watched James for a split second as he bellowed from the window, 'James, James!' It was no good. James was totally transfixed and locked into a daze.

James was in a trance and was unable to hear Tom yelling out.

Realising that James was in some sort of spellbinding trance, Tom took in a gulp of air and in anticipation glanced over to the tree and into the sun's rays; in that second Tom comprehended

The Dream Catcher

he would have to sprint to restrain James from entering the small clearing being eaten by the tall towering tree.

He shouted again from the top of his voice through the opened window, 'James, wait up! Don't do it!'

There was no response. Tom didn't wait for a further response. He just scurried as quickly as he could down the stairs, knocking some pictures hanging in the hallway as he grabbed his rucksack and rushed into the street and across the path where the light source shone brightly, and the large, overpowering tree seemed to be smothering James.

As Tom got closer to James, again he shouted, 'James!'

Tom grabbed James's arm, and questioned strongly, 'James, what are you doing?' Tom quickened his pace to keep up with his brother.

But James just turned his head and with a steely glare continued walking into the arms or what appeared to be branches of the strange tree.

'James, where are you going?' Tom was anxious and petrified of the outcome.

Tom queried again, puzzled, glaring at his brother with his turned-up lip and incredulous frown in his brow. Tom was now wearily looking around, fearing that Morkann or her army of Ghouls would appear. James just glanced wildly at Tom, silently blinking his eyes and looking straight ahead then continuing to walk into the large tree arms.

Although the walk was but a short distance it felt like hours had passed. All Tom could do was to try and stop James from walking further.

Tom's mind whizzed — he was not aware of any other entrance to the galaxies apart from the boiler room. But he did know that

James was being force-led and was unsure to whom or where he was heading. Was it to the Galaxy? And more importantly, was this character Hakeem of goodness or was he bad?

Tom presumed James was now being led to the Galaxy through another entrance than that through the boiler room at school, so where was James walking to? And more importantly who was behind it? Or what was behind it? Who or what was leading him to where? Tom tried to recall all the characters he had met in Oblivionarna previously.

Tom bellowed, panicking, 'James!' Again there was no response, just a steely stare.

James kept on walking in a hypnotic trance.

Then as Tom and James seemed to be swallowed up by the light source in the tree, a voice broke out.

'I have been waiting for you—come,' it bellowed in a deep, magnetic voice.

James caught a glimpse of something in the clearing as he peered into a tall, overwhelming figure in the distance mingling and entwined in the strange tree, which was seeping through the branches with the leaves dazzling and twinkling like autumn emeralds with burnt-orange, topaz droplets. As he gazed deep into the tree he was able to make out a huge, tall, muscular, pronounced figure draped in what looked like a Monk's robe. James locked his eyes in to the figure in the tree until his eyes became waterlogged.

The extremely tall, towering, muscular figure stood as tall as the Redwood Coast tree itself. He was draped in a crystal robe shimmering like diamonds in the sun's rays, resembling that of a Gregorian Monk. His face was powerful and could not be seen, for his hood fell over his head making him appear as a faceless creature

The Dream Catcher

except for his piercing, penetrating, dark, hard eyes seeping through his visage which appeared like voids—chasms where one would be lost. His mouth was strong with no frown. He had a mighty torso with strong arms that could hold an army, yet the façade of the tree covered his power. His hands were fierce yet he used them gently when encouraging both boys to walk closer.

In one hand he held the bright light source, which flickered out like a flame. He had used this to beckon James, who, although totally transfixed, walked on wide-eyed, looming with fear.

The flame flickering was known as Hayley's Star. This was the star which held all Lost Dreams, and Hakeem held it bravely.

The faceless, tall, dark figure draped in a Monk's shimmering crystal robe was engulfed in a radiance of an aura of a sudden, white, bright light. The light source which surrounded him was so angelic that Tom was also mesmerised by the glow alone. His penetrating, dark, piercing eyes shone wide like open chasms and were pronounced.

This was Hakeem, the bearer of all that was good, from the land of Oblivionarna. Tom grabbed James's arm and, now convinced of who this character was, tried to tell James.

'James, stop! Do you know who he is? Shall I tell you?' he asked wearily, trying desperately to convince him not to walk on. But James did not stop walking and was totally locked in a trance. Tom was now apprehensive. He was worried about James pacing so close to the character he had only heard of. He knew there was something special about Hakeem—what was it? He was puzzled. All Tom could think of was why James had taken the hoop with beads from the spider's web, which he had found at the entrance of where this colossal tree was standing. Tom began to wish Jambalee was with him and how he was needed so much now.

Hayley's Star

'If he was here, it would be just so cool, and he would know what to do,' Tom muttered to himself, still peering and watching helplessly from the bedroom window. "I know Jambalee would be able to get hold of James. He would stop him. If only he had a mobile phone?" he thought to himself sarcastically.

He patted his jacket pocket making sure that he had put the magic white powder pouch safely together with the liquid in the small flask into the pocket. These were items Jambalee had given him.

After an initial brief gaze, both Tom and James took a closer look with their wide-open, bedazzled eyes in trepidation as if a bullet had has just shot past them. They were petrified, and did not know if the figure was a friend or foe.

Hakeem lived in the Palace of Greatness, and it was known that he was the only one who was able to solve the mystery of all Lost Dreams. Hence he would carry Hayley's Star and protect the dreams which could be made real. James and Tom were totally in awe of this magnificent being.

Then as James approached closer and within grasping reach of Hakeem, the light flickered intently more like a gas flame so as to cast an orange bright glow across James's face. Both boys now gazed into the abyss of Hakeem's eyes in sheer terror.

Tom quickly glanced over at James and watched how his face plummeted in horror, not knowing how the events would manifest it.

As both boys fell into the shadow of Hakeem's robe, Hakeem slowly lifted his branch-covered arms, still holding the flame of Haley's Star flickering strongly. Hakeem was able to create a powerful surge in a spectrum of fire flames, and with one quick blast of energy Hakeem sucked in both boys. James and Tom were

The Dream Catcher

now engulfed into a sudden fireball which erupted with a great boom.

The flames which rode on Hakeem's arm quickly transformed into a ball of wild fire as if a comet had engulfed them. Hakeem was now in control, and both boys were blasted into the atmosphere at great speed. Everything was quick, too quick for James or Tom to exhale or take in a breath of air. Everything happened at great velocity.

The pressure from the wind blew against both James and Tom, and as their faces became compressed their cheeks became red and puffed out thus making their eyes squint and waterlogged. A spectrum of bright orange, yellow, and pink flames burned ferociously — it was a raging fireball. This was it; maybe this was how Hayley's Star was created? It was how Hayley's Star had transformed into Hayley's Comet! Their thoughts darted around just as quickly as they travelled in this amazing ball of fire.

They could not believe it, for now they realized they were both heading for the galaxies as they ascended high up into the air at such velocity. Tom tried to look at his brother as James held on tightly; his knuckles became red and sore as the rage of wind slapped his hands, slicing each knuckle bone to exit his hand. James still grabbed onto the hoop with the beads covered in a silver spider's web.

Everything whizzed past the boys as they flew higher into the atmosphere, swooping past houses and zooming higher then higher into the soft, misty, dove clouds of different shapes. The atmosphere then suddenly became dark, cold, and abruptly solemn. Hakeem and the boys zipped past floating comets of odd shapes and colours zooming through the galactic air-space until they had completely disappeared into an abyss, a dark void atmosphere to an

unknown land. Hakeem, still holding the rage of fire surrounding the boys, slowed the pace, and both James and Tom could feel the intensity simmer. The boys closed their eyes while Hakeem used his other hand to cast a white, transparent shield around them. As he lifted his arm a great shadow was cast. Tom glared at his new surroundings while James was still locked in a trance. Hakeem had given them air to breathe before their transition and resting place in the planet of Oblivionarna.

Chapter II

This chapter includes Latin

The Hoop with Feathers

As Hakeem descended, both Tom and James reflected on how they had travelled and who this strange character was. They were scared, and they were a very long way from home. The boys could not speak; they were frozen with fear etched upon their faces. James, still in a trance, pondered all the new encounters that he had made previously on his rescue mission and what he would now discover.

As the conundrum zoomed around James's mind he could only think of the beautiful princess who had captured his heart and whom he had met and rescued. He remembered her amazing voice and how it locked all into a trance and even made the tower crumble. Then there was the tiny tenacious Halaconia and her strange captivating appearance. It was, however, odd that he should think of these strange creatures in this very strange predicament.

The boys were holding firmly onto Hakeem's fire-fuelled arm. They were petrified until the bright yellow and orange fireball flames slowly faded, disintegrating away, and in its place it left a hazy, orange glow. Hakeem descended, gliding over a ravine of a

The Dream Catcher

rocky gauge and an open basin of mountainous, arduous, isolated terrain. They could see the galaxy clearly now as they began to glide and descend into the land of Oblivionarna. The fireball slowly began to diminish, and Hayley's burning bright star returned, flickering gently as the light began to glow. Hakeem then opened his arm and released two very frightened boys into the galaxy. James was the first to disembark out of Hakeem's grip, and Tom followed.

Still within a shell of light around them, Hakeem bellowed in Latin, *'Vos ero tutus hic insquequo Jambalee reverto, is mos rector vos! James—habitum in angustus ut hoop quod don't permissum quisquam take is vobis—comprehendo. Xle-Ha.'*

'Yeah, what did he say? Your Latin is better than mine, tell me!' Tom said anxiously.

'You will be safe here until Jambalee returns. He will guide you! James—hold on tightly to the hoop and don't let anyone take it from you—including Xle-Ha!'

James repeated each word and then questioned Tom. 'Tom, that's what he said.' James was relieved by his translation. 'The thing is, Xle-Ha. I mean, who is he? There are some strange characters on this land, Tom!' James exclaimed wearily.

'I know, you'll get used to it, but I don't know who Xle-Ha is. I have never met him!' You still have that hoop though, don't you?' Tom asked in anguish.

James snatched at his pocket and took out the hoop, peering intently at the beads, which were threaded through horse-hair. They shimmered gently lifting to waft in the cool breeze.

'Do you know, I thought this hoop looked like a bird initially,' grimaced James.

James gazed up at the faceless Hakeem trying to see his visage, but he was too tall and the smoke created a screen which was not penetrable. James looked at Tom hoping he would know who Xle-Ha was—he did not. So James turned back to face Hakeem through the smoke screen as Tom shrugged his shoulders blankly.

Once the boys had landed, they took their cautious first steps into the desolate land; the sky had become a green mist together with a spectrum of colours that formed the entrance to the Palace of Greatness. It was clear to see the opulence and grandeur of an impressive site. They walked closer into the terrain as Hakeem followed, guiding the two boys in his shadow.

Both boys gazed on in astonishment as the tall, towering, powerful figure of Hakeem approached the gates of the palace. James could see the white mosaic marble fountain which greeted them dripping dew drops of silver liquid emulating mercury, which then floated in bulbs of silver onto the muted saffron colours of the mosaic tray below.

As they peered closer both Tom and James were able to see abhorrent, giant-like fish; they were odd and on closer inspection appeared unfriendly. These swimming bloodcurdling creatures had large, obtruding, blue, dazzling, diamond eyes and a wide mouth hiding its razor-sharp teeth. It had golden scales with a smooth front, and its fins were helping it to slide slowly as it slithered through silver, slimy liquid emulating mercury, which was being collected in the mosaic marble tray of the fountain. Alone and confused, Tom nudged James's elbow eagerly.

'Look!' he barked, pointing to the creatures swimming. James stared attentively down into the fountain; as he gawped intently watching these strange-looking creatures slide and whirl he became mesmerised with their strange pattern of swimming. James realised very quickly that the fish were not just ordinary fish, but it was the evil Morkann in disguise.

The Dream Catcher

James frowned and peered back at his brother. 'Come on, we have got to get out here!' he snapped.

James gawped in terror at the abhorrent fish, how they raged and jumped out of and then back into the fountain, which led into a deep sonata of sounds. Every splash created gave an uneven ripple—something was not quite right. Their piercing eyes and the strange green fin from one of fish would dart out like a misplaced hair. The strange fish continued in their swim, and there did not seem to be any pattern except for their robotic glide in the silver, gleaming liquid. James was not able to recognise any of the fish which swam or even if they were fish, for they appeared too loathsome and ferocious. James and Tom were both petrified and dared not gaze at these frightening creatures in fear for their lives.

As both boys glared in horror, there was a sudden splash, a torrent of liquid which sprayed everywhere, covering most of the area and the marble mosaic floor outside the fountain with a large towering wave that glided into the air and zoomed across the fountain at great speed.

Tom glared in deep apprehension at something that darted across his eyes at great speed. It appeared so quickly, and then just vanished. It was in a silver shadow form, like a dolphin-type creature only larger. It appeared almost solid, shiny silver. It suddenly rushed through the liquid causing white water to spill over on to the mosaic marble floor. Then the strange fish realised that the silver shadow had arrived to oust them.

'Hey, do you see that?' Tom asked James as he scaled the fountain for the strange, large, silver fish creature.

James turned to his brother with an unbelieving look. 'Just answer me this!' James bellowed again. 'Do freshwater fish and saltwater fish flow from the same stream?'

'What? Not just now!' insisted a puzzled Tom. 'No—yes—I don't know right now. That creature, whatever it was, was more than I want to share—huge and even scarier! Why are you asking?!' Tom was unsure of why he was being questioned.

Again James turned to his brother and asked again curiously whilst watching out for the malicious fish, 'Tom, can both freshwater and saltwater fish flow from the same spring?'

James was intent on finding the answer, but it seemed Tom did not know and he was frightened.

The boys tried to make sense of the strange happenings, but James knew the Christian Bible talked about good over evil and James was trying to piece together, in his own unique way, if the fish types were really Morkann in disguise, like some shape-shifter creature, and the silver fish were really the goodness of the palace.

The abhorrent fish jumped up out the fountain with their mouths open wide and their teeth pointing like daggers in anticipation for a kill at the boys'. It was apparent that these were no ordinary fish, if fish at all. They tried to lunge at the boys, jumping up and quickly causing havoc and mayhem in the fountain.

The liquid splashed everywhere, and both Tom and James slid onto the liquid in their struggle to get away from the devil-like creatures. Both Tom and James ducked to avoid their razor-sharp, icicle teeth, and each time the fish dived forward they tried to catch a bite of the boys. The boys dived and ducked away sliding on the mayhem left behind. As each swipe of the fish jumped for a kill, they would lunge forward with their wide-open mouths, displaying their scalpel-type teeth. They snarled and glared and were attempting to hurt the boys. Again Morkann's plot failed—Hakeem had protected the boys.

The Dream Catcher

The fish then took position and tried to hide from the silver shadow. As they did, the silver shadow manoeuvred in great speed and with what appeared to be a tail or large fin he began to stir up the silt from the magnificent fountain. The silver shadow had created a v-shape trap of silt and mud. The abhorrent fish had nowhere to go except into the cleverly created trap. The hideous fish would only now be caught in the jaws of the giant silver shadow.

Suddenly it happened, and both boys gazed in terror. The sudden splashes of white-cloud bubbles dancing and jumping out of the large fountain marble base were the tell-tale signs along with the screams and deafening screeching cry as loud as a rocket launcher of a hundred decibels piercing and slicing the air in a wild pot of bubbles. The noise was piercing and was endlessly absorbed with the image of the ferocious narcissistic fish. The fish were so proud and so malevolent and now they had just disappeared.

As they did so the shadow or creature appeared to smile at the boys, giving no time to receive a smile back from either boy. Just as quick as it had appeared it disappeared and faded into the liquid. Both boys were baffled at what they'd seen.

Tom slowly yet nervously looked up at James. He licked his lips, in fear and with a forlorn gaze. Tom hesitated to answer James's interesting question but before he could he could answer they heard a tumultuous, sudden, loud noise coming from the other side of the fountain. The noise became louder and more aggressive.

Hakeem peered at both boys. He could see what was happening. As he lifted his large hand, the fish saw the dark shadow appear and then they disappeared disintegrating like silver fish slithering into a crevice.

Hakeem hollered, 'You are safe now. You must go and take hold of your land—there is not much time!' And with that, the

The Hoop with Feathers

huge, faceless, muscular, robed being stomped away and with him the flicker of Hayley's Star faded into the distance.

Both boys were astonished and frightened; they were now left in a wilderness and a palace which seemed to have swallowed them up.

The Palace of Greatness was now in sheer darkness, and all that could be heard was the slow heavy trickle, drop by drop, of the silver mercury-type liquid dripping from the mouth of the fountain over the ridge as it fell onto the marble ornate floor. The flames on the torches crackled in either side of the palace, as they stood proud guarding its entrance.

James looked on, and Tom glared with baited breath, licking his lips as his eyes opened wide in fear like a nocturnal creature. His body was still unable to move held back in fear. Tom looked over at James; in forlorn despair both of them were now petrified and unaware on how to get out the palace.

Tom could only think of Jambalee and was hoping, longing he would come to their rescue or even the Dillyan, Halaconia. James then continued to wonder about his surroundings and where he was being led by whom. The boys slowly stepped forward through the strange shadows past the fountain. They could see a strange jungle-like path in the distance but it was heavily covered. They hear sounds like that of nocturnal life begging to wake up. They wearily trudged on as the path slowly disappeared. It wrapped itself around benign and mangled twigs of a land unknown. In the distance the boys could see the trees beckoning them to walk closer. Its snarled, twisted, enormous, lone, angry trunks seemed to tear up the ground. As the night fell, it was apparent that the lonely land had come to life.

The stars twinkled and glistened forming a constellation like that of an arcade full of colorful bright lights held in a void called

The Dream Catcher

space. Tom could clearly hear the chitterling of innocuous sounds twittering in the cold, callous air bouncing off from misshaped comets floating into the arctic airspace.

The night air was heavy with the stench of stagnant, dank, decomposing silt dripping from random rocks floating in the galactic airspace. Drooping old vines swayed in their path as if they were in a serpents' lair.

The odor was so overpowering, both boys began to hold up their noses, feeling sick and nauseous at the stench. The boys had no choice but to continue their pensive, arduous pacing along the soaked grey mud in search of the warm glow flickering in the hope they would find Hakeem and the right path!

They continued with their journey, stumbling on vicious thorns which in turn seemed to glare out at both boys in the hope they would fail in their quest. Tom stared into the horizon, in disarray, his eyes wide open like that of an awakening bat. In the anticipation of seeing Hakeem or Halaconia—anyone who could help them through the dark terrain. James and Tom slowly and cautiously took their stride.

Tom let out a heavy sigh and wondered in anguish, 'Argh, how much more?' He looked up James. 'Are you okay?'

Tom was petrified and almost felt uneasy as he pursued his brother still locked in a semi-mesmerized trance. However, he realised very quickly that they both would not be able to turn back and would have to continue. Tom turned around to face James.

'James, do you have the hoop?' he bellowed in hope.

James looked down into his jacket pocket feeling for the hoop before yanking it out from its safe place and then replying with a steely expression, 'Yes I have got it—it's here!'

The Hoop with Feathers

'Good!' a relieved Tom replied. 'You are going to need it soon.' Tom peered intently whilst gazing around the galactic space. 'We have got to be very careful, or we could end up in The Valley of Tongues!' he yelped.

His voice reverberated around the galaxy bouncing off each of the large colorful constellations together with the floating pitted rocks. James turned sharply and looked up, wide-eyed and full of fear, staring into the horizon in front of him. Scared for his life, he turned to face Tom with a sullen sunken face.

'You do know, I am petrified—you do know that!' Revealed James, screwing up his eyes and glancing over at Tom in trepidation.

'And what are you talking about the Valley of Tongues?' questioned a weary James.

The bright beam of light was now flickering from the luminous, golden-orange flames guarding the entrance to the grand majestic palace, and both boys knew they would have to go and find Hakeem as well their way to rescue the princess and be able to protect themselves in this perfidious terrain.

'So where has that THING gone then?' queried James to Tom.

'What thing?' asked Tom.

'You know that tree— and the fireball."

'That THING,' Tom said, 'happens to be Hakeem, the bearer of all lost dreams. Jambalee told me the story about him...he is quite an elusive character.'

Tom had relinquished all the information he could to James.

James looked up and seemed to be very busy contemplating how to get out of the palace and find his way home.

'Ehmm,' James mumbled.

Tom was unsure whether James understood what he had done.

The Dream Catcher

'I don't know who that giant was, but he was kind of weird!' James yelped.

'But right now we have to get out of here.'

James continued to look at the fountain, watching the giant newt-like creatures swim ferociously in what appeared to be a mercury-filled marble fountain.

But before Tom engaged in a conversation and debated what James had muttered, the two boys heard some obscure strange noises echoing through the palace. They panicked and hid quietly, irrationally ducking below the marble fountain ridge.

Tom gestured to James to be quiet and not to move or say anything. He then quickly glanced down at the abhorrent, giant, newt-type creatures splashing and swimming, in the silver thick mercury-filled liquid. They had suddenly stopped and now appeared still and lifeless floating on the silver mercury drops.

James looked up and quizzed Tom with a hushed voice, 'Look! There's your answer!'

He whispered, pointing to the newts floating on the surface. James continued to watch the creatures which petrified him. James was fascinated with their size and the way the fish lay completely still.

Still staring in disbelief, James watched intently as he reached out to Tom. Then suddenly there was a large splash and a booming roar, as if a Tsunami had just occurred. The hideous fish let out the most deafening of splashes of evil and iniquity seethed from their large obtruding eyes. Tom could clearly see the perilous happenings, yet he suddenly became as still as a statue whilst still trying to stretch out his ear listening hard to the strange wailing.

He could hear Morkann wailing in the distance with the noise of swishing muslin gowns wafting and swaying to a rhythmic wild breeze. They seemed to be conversing in Latin.

The Hoop with Feathers

Tom peered over to James. 'Tell me what they are saying," he mimed, gesturing with his hands discreetly so as not to be seen.

James looked on intently, hushing Tom to be quiet, so that he could get a good listen.

'Nos must reperio lemma ("we must find them").' He then turned to Tom.

James translated, slowly repeating each word almost phonetically.

'Crikey!' James murmured, afraid of what was being suggested by whoever's voice he was now able to hear. He turned to Tom, tilting his head up straight and staring into the top of the fountain. 'We have got to find Jambalee!' he stated quite firmly, 'and get out of this place.'

Tom nodded slowly and nervously, their eyes both open wide in fear. As they both carefully began to wonder off into the palace their footsteps echoed on the great, cold, marble floor. Neither Tom nor James said anything. They couldn't—they were too frightened to even mutter a syllable.

Then they saw the first light creeping across the distance through the majestic window frames, peaking beneath a chasm. The boys walked on wearily. A chill ran through their bones, and their arms and hands became ice cold. Knowing this, Tom looked up at James frowning and dipping his eyes as they became waterlogged. For the first time, Tom, although he had frequented the galaxy before was petrified, and now totally unsure of his surroundings.

James tried to reassure Tom. 'Don't worry!' he muttered, trying to calm him and knowing he was scared. 'Just come on. We don't have much time.'

He hurriedly pulled Tom to walk on further. Apprehensively Tom walked, gazing at his new surroundings with steely eyes. James peered over at Tom nervously, anxious about the next step.

The Dream Catcher

'I think they are in here—they must be.' James was sure the noises were heard from this spot.

The chill in the palace became colder; the frostiness was beginning to feel like sudden death. The boys glared at each other with a forlorn look. It became unbearable—so much so that as both Tom and James were walking they could feel their hands aching and becoming numb with the sudden icy temperatures.

They walked on towards the light peaking through the window frames. It bounced back from the stone walls and onto the ornate marble mosaic floor. Tom was sure this was a sign, a sign of where Morkann could be lurking under a disguise. She was a devious, venomous creature and could shape-shift into anything. Tom led the way along a narrow corridor, the bright light dazzling and playing games of hit-and-miss on the cold silent walls surrounding the old stairs.

'Well, is she here?' James nervously asked Tom, his voice echoing in the palace.

'I don't-know right now,' Tom answered wearily. He followed James slowly, full of terror

There were so many questions darting inside James's head; should he stay and use the magic pouch to pursue his conflict with the Ghouls and Morkann whom he was petrified of, or should he wander into the vast terrain of wonderment accompanying Tom in search for Jambalee and discover his princess? All that he had longed for was to meet his initial rescue, Princess Anna Lisa.

It felt like a difficult choice. However, James slowly led the way through the palace, his footsteps echoing on the cold, mosaic, marble slabs as the shadows grew from his small footprints. In his anticipation he could only think of the princess whom he had rescued and how beautiful she was. He contemplated the things he would say to her should he ever see her again. How would he approach her?

Both Boys searched for an opening out of the palace. They walked onto the terrain cautiously. Tom led the way taking small steps, cautiously wandering into the grand opening of white marble flooring. The rays from the dome window above shone rays of stars onto the cold, marble walls forming abstract images. The fountain flowing with mercury drops trickled and echoed through the palace room. Both boys turned in amazement to look and view the images of the shapes appearing on the dimmed marble wall. James glanced over at the newt-like fish jumping out at him from the mercury-filled fountain.

The eyes of the newt-type fish were protruding now wide open and gruesome. They appeared like golf balls, and their mouths displayed their razor-sharp teeth. The teeth slowly transformed into fangs that appeared as vicious as if a piranha and shark had mated together to form these obnoxious creatures. The boys quivered in fear. James was glued to watching these ugly creatures. He could see the pupils of these now-monstrous newt-type creatures glooming down at him. The boys stared back at the fish. In horror their mouths dropped open, but they were unable to scream. They froze for a split second. Their eyes glared at the mercury, alien, newt-type fish in wonderment. Tom began to slowly and robotically look for the magic powder pouch from his pocket.

'James, watch out!' screamed Tom as the blue newt jumped out of the mercury-filled fountain splashing thick droplets of silver mercury everywhere. The creature then lunged up at him. The fish had grown and magnified into a zombiefied Garble fish.

It was horrendous, and Tom was still desperately searching for the pouch, frantically pulling at every angle at his jacket.

The Dream Catcher

'Where is it?' he angrily questioned himself, becoming very frustrated with his lack of progress. 'James, it looks like mercury—I can't quite be sure though—that's what this liquid is!'

'How do you stop mercury?' James asked anxiously. 'Quick, come on, tell me before they jump out again and kill us!'

Tom had had a brain wave; before James could answer, Tom found the powder after delving for several minutes into his jacket pocket, which felt like a good couple of hours. He then wrenched it out of his pocket as quick as he could and threw some grains over the ugly obtruding fish.

James watched in horror. Realising the fish were still trying to attack them, he desperately pulled Tom out of the way as the large ugly obtruding fish tried to lunge forward and attack both of the boys. Tom screamed, and James had sweat dripping in rivulets down his face. James was panicking and didn't know which tool he should use.

Tom knew that the pouch containing the magic powder would stop the fish in its tracks. His eyes were dropped as he realised how close both boys had come to meeting death. He had one eye on the creature and the other on his brother and himself. He was stunned and could not think of anything other than to find the pouch that Jambalee had given him.

Tom yelped, 'We have to get out of here,' as the malevolent, malicious fish jumped up at both boys, their hideous, fuming, fiery eyes burning with rage.

'Quick, follow me,' Tom bellowed.

Tom glared at James, frowning as he manically searched for the pouch containing the magic powder. Fumbling through his trouser pockets he managed to feel the pouch and then yanked it out. He let our a yell and hurriedly threw some of the powder onto the fish.

The Hoop with Feathers

'What will that do?' asked James anxiously, panicking at the enormous size of these mysterious creatures.

The fish seemed to take to the air like birds of prey. Their eyes were deep and menacing. They seemed to be able to follow the boys around the grand marble vestibule.

The mercury dribbled onto the floor, releasing silver mammoth drops as large as an ostrich eggs forming colossal mountain peaks.

The boys started running, darting anywhere on the cold, bright, marble floor as the mercury drops cascaded, falling over the fountain ridge. Slowly each drip bounced off the floor, and the fish became larger and larger almost like ninja monster fish from hell.

They ran past the brightly lit torches on the walls, causing silky shadows to dance in various shapes from translucent images. The distorted shapes seemed to come alive, melting into the darkness as the boys hurriedly ran turning each corner down the wooden spiral staircase. The boys were wide-eyed and petrified, frightened in every bone. James could feel his hair on his neck standing proud as his lips quivered. Tom watched intently the strange obscure figures dancing against the cold marble walls in silky silhouettes. Wide-eyed with fear etched upon his face, Tom held his sword tightly, thinking about how he was to leave this unknown land.

Tom ran past James and squealed, 'Look over here!' He pointed to an opening which seemed to lead into a courtyard and then into the palace grounds. Tom gulped in a deep breath and took all his strength to lunge forward into the old huge Iron Gate before them.

The journey through the dense terrain against the odds had drained Tom but he knew he was to assist James. They could now hear Morkann's Ghouls sounding their menacing sounds and hollering around the stagnant air. Both boys were now outside but still on the palace grounds. The strange fish in mercury water suddenly leaped up at them as they marched on through the grounds.

The Dream Catcher

James could see the fear looming in Tom's eyes. He took Tom's sword by the hilt and swiped the large sword at the repugnant head, piercing the open mouth laden with dagger-sharp, white teeth trying to grab him.

'Argh!' he shouted. James ran slashing at the fish trying to hurt him. A brownish red liquid slowly oozed out of the scales and then trickled down the fish falling onto the sword which James was still holding. James watched, quivering, waiting for the fish to stop. It did not; it appeared enraged and angry that James had even considered trying to kill it.

'Get your—get your powder again—it needs more, Tom!' James bellowed. 'Quickly!'

The fish were now jumping and attacking both boys. Tom and James struggled to fight the fish, and then James pulled out his hoop with feathers. Not really knowing how to use the instrument, he hailed it into the air, waving it about over each fish.

Then there was a pause suddenly. After a short while the large fish stopped jumping up at both boys, and James could see there was a sudden difference in their behaviour, so he used the hoop again waving in the air several times.

Tom, seeing the hoop was working, shouted out and took back the sword from James so that he could concentrate on using his hoop.

'Keep doing that,' Tom bellowed.

Tom slashed the air with the sword fighting back the fish. James continued wafting the hoop, and, sure enough, the fish abruptly stopped.

'Phew, what the...' James wiped his brow, and glared down at the hoop in his hand.

'Come on, we better get out of here,' Tom said.

The Hoop with Feathers

'Yeah!' Both boys tried to catch their breath back as they trudged through the terrain now covered in silver mercury. James was still shaken and in deep thought.

'It's a good thing you don't come here too often!' James said, peering down at the ground.

Tom realised that the instrument which James had used was a very powerful tool.

Both boys trudged further deeper into the dark terrain, passed the prairie of obscure, shaped crystals hanging from mushroom vines. James could see a minute light through the dark land. Pausing he turned to his brother. 'Look, what is that?' he asked, pointing hopefully.

Tom glared over at the light source James was pointing to. 'Okay, lets follow it, then.' Frowning, Tom let James lead the way.

They walked on their feet creating craters in the mushy land. Tom looked around wearily and nervously. Suddenly a large labyrinthine ravine appeared and they heard a screaming noise which etched the air with a spine-chilling shudder.

Tom and James looked at each other; they walked closer together and walked on slowly until they could see the light source more clearly.

James held out his hoop, anticipating something terrible would appear.

Tom and James ran fast into the deep, dense terrain and whizzed passed the wild rock branches strewn across the ground. Tripping over the fallen bracken they zipped past the bowing trees where James knocked his head. Feeling unsteady, James cupped his forehead as they sped through a labyrinth, across the Tor, to the banks of what appeared to be a great ravine with a sudden drop.

The Dream Catcher

Tom grabbed a branch and slapped the trickling water three times. Out of the swirling chaos rose what appeared to be a giant crocodile monster with a mouth wide enough to take Tom in one gulp. A row of white ivory daggers appeared as snow-capped mountains proudly positioned on the Valley of the Moons gaped in a menacing grin, The small, bloodshot eyes of the hungry monster serpent recognised Tom, his prey. In one of the heads the jaws were clamped shut. His heads, of which there were many, a hundred at least, smashed the ground in search of his long awaited prey—Tom, and the other.

Typhoeusina could now see that they were two, Tom and of course the meatier morsel, James. The monster swung his heads like an acrobatic dancer whirling and swirling his long, svelte, strong necks above its head that roared like a thousand tigers. Then he shook one of his heads and the silver water dazzled and shimmered, rippling and rolling in the mercury-filled ravine. The monster let out a tumultuous rage; Tom recognized only too well that this monster could kill in one swipe of his laser tongues, which were a green slime colour covered with abhorrent protruding sore spores. A hundred heads slammed and splashed at the mercury water. It was Typhoeusina, and she was back with a vengeance! Her eyes beamed large as a lighthouse, bright, menacing, and searching for her blood hunger.

'James, we have got to go from here…leave now!' yelled Tom.

Tom ran as fast as he could, searching his pocket for the magic powder. He had to do something. Tom was in sheer terror, unsure whether he should even contemplate throwing the powder onto this massive monsterous creature.

James, petrified, stopped running, and with a forlorn look hid behind a large broken boulder. Thinking he would not be seen, he

The Hoop with Feathers

panted anxiously as the sweat trickled in rivulets over his face and neck. His hands became red and clammy; he glared with his open eyes wide transfixed on the serpent's sudden movements.

'Tom, do you know this THING?' barked James to Tom as he tried to catch his breath. The monster serpent glared deviously and snapped its razor-sharp jaws, as red and orange flares flew out and a fireball erupted. His thick, scaly skin, automatically became covered in a slime of heat, making each scale visible. Tom glared at the menacing creature and very carefully threw some of the powder onto his tail which slid across the ground like a slithering anaconda snake.

Tom's face dipped. He was petrified, shocked, and very scared, but he had to help his brother. 'James, when I say run, you gotta run—right?'

James gave a nervous acknowledgment and got ready to run from his newfound hiding place. Tom carefully and inconspicuously began the search for the magic powder he had put into his bag without being seen.

'Yeah, are you okay? Now just run,' Tom answered as he in trepidation agitatedly tried to locate his powder from the bag.

'What the—?' James sneered over at the monster. Typhoeusina was so large that it was difficult to see all of its limbs and to establish how large it actually was. As both boys were running for dear life James yelled, 'Tom, quickly jump over that boulder and duck!'

James, not wanting to lose his brother, shouted back, 'But you?'

'Just do as I say!' replied an anxious Tom.

As both boys ran Tom could feel each head and each pair of topaz eyes glaring at him and his brother. Tom still searched frantically in his pockets and found his powder. He pulled put out the packet and proudly announced, 'Come on then!' He beckoned

The Dream Catcher

the monster, teasing it with powder. Then a head lunged forward and Tom threw powder granules onto one of the huge serpents' neck. He wasn't sure if anything would happen as they were just too many of them.

James dived behind a large molten boulder on the grey muddy terrain. As he did so Tom threw some of the white magic powder into Typhoeusina's eyes. Tom at that moment was unclear which eye or which face or which part of raging monster had been struck with the powder. He prayed that it would work.

'Come on…work, work, come on… please…please,' Tom stammered under his breath.

'Don't you have a gun or something!?' shouted James. A worried James chased after Tom to tell him to hide or duck from the monster's glare.

'Don't worry, James, I know it's scary, I've seen it before!' replied Tom

Then Tom found his moment. He lent forward and ever so carefully threw randomly five drops onto the tail of the monster. Tom didn't know whether it was the same tail or multiple tails except that he was sure it had been hit with the powder.

James watched intensely, his eyes open wide, panting deeply, when suddenly a tumultuous noise was heard, and with a loud thunder one large, long, thick, scaly neck fell crashing to the ground. It rolled down and slumped into a crater, and in doing so the monster lost its balance and plunged onto a crater causing the planet to shudder like a tyrant magma earthquake had just occurred.

The monster knew his time had passed, and he was defeated. He roared and bellowed and buckled with each limb and then he released a sorrowful groan and then with a thundering crash it fell. Everything shuddered.

James called out to Tom. They felt a sudden rush of relief. Both boys trudged on deeper into the terrain peering through the foliage and rocks for any glimpse of Jambalee or Hakeem. They hoped that they would see anyone who could be of help to them. They ran and scuttled through the unfamiliar territory.

The path slowly disappeared as it wrapped itself around the benign and mangled twigs of a land unknown. Its snarled, twisted, enormous, lone, angry trunks seemed to tear at the rugged tor. As night fell, it was apparent that the land had come to life.

The blue stars twinkled so sharply, appearing as if they were going to fall from the void where they cautiously balanced. They glistened, forming a constellation like that of an arcade full of colorful bright lights telling a story of secrets long forgotten held in a void called space. Tom could clearly hear the clanking of innocuous sounds twittering in the cold, callous, cosmos air bouncing off from misshaped comets floating into the arctic airspace.

The night air was heavy with the stench of stagnant, dank, decomposing silt dripping from random rocks floating in the galactic airspace.

The odour was so overpowering that both boys began to hold up their noses, feeling sick and nauseous at the stench. The boys had no choice but to continue their pensive, arduous pacing along the soaked grey mud in search for the bright glow flickering in the hope they would find Hakeem!

They continued with their journey stumbling on vicious thorns, disused rocks, and bracken which in turn seemed to glare out at both boys in the hope they would fail in their quest. Tom stared into the horizon, his raccoon flashbulb eyes and dilated pupils were wide open like a nocturnal creature in the anticipation they would

The Dream Catcher

see a friendly face—Hakeem, Halaconia, anyone that could help them through the dark dense terrain.

James took in a deep gulp of air; in anguish his lungs filled with the callous, cold, crisp air around him.

'Argh, how much more?' James was tiring and his limbs were sore. He glanced over at his brother. 'Tom, are you okay?'

Tom nodded, knowing he would just have to continue following.

Tom was terrified. He felt uneasy following his brother in a trance; Tom was completely mesmerised but tried in vain to fight the robotic control as he still walked on pursuing his brother. However, he knew they both were unable to turn back and would have to continue.

"We have got to get out of here quickly, or we could end up in The Valley of Tongues!' he yelped.

His voice reverberated around the galaxy bouncing off from each large brightly coloured constellation. James sharply looked up, wide-eyed and full of fear, staring into the horizon in front; he turned sharply to face Tom with a sullen sunken face as he grimaced. When he reached the top of the path, his hands became sore and were still trembling.

'She has got to be here,' he whispered to himself, thinking of Princess Anna Lisa. But somehow his thought came alive, and Tom heard his passion.

I know who you're thinking of,' shouted Tom as he frowned. 'Come on, she can't be far!' He was by now totally confused. He was also fed-up and totally tired of the trudging through the barren land and found no reason why he should continue.

Chapter III
The Valley of Tongues

This chapter includes Latin

The boys carefully scaled the rugged pitted rocks and bare terrain; they could sense the uneasiness as they slowly trudged on wearily, glancing at their new surroundings. They nervously peered out at the strange landscape, made up of serene colours and textures of marshland with an abundance of mountainous, rugged rocks with floating gem-coloured comets. Tom and James could see the brightly colored comets shooting past in the distance. In the vastness of where the boys had found themselves there was a haze, a smoke in the distance, which seemed to lure the boys in what seemed a hypnotic trance. It was strange that both boys were now transfixed into a galaxy that appeared to have locked their very existence and totally engulfed them into a hologram of light. James felt a cold shiver shudder through his spine. His hands became clammy and suddenly turned ice-cold. James looked up in a steely expression of pure determination to continue in this strange of strangest lands; he stepped up and paced on, hoping he would find Hakeem.

The Dream Catcher

The boys trudged on. As they did in the dark, cold, solemn air something was following them—something unknown, something unseen, and something too horrific to capture a glimpse of.

Tom whispered hesitantly, quickly grabbing James's forearm. He nervously looked up at Tom, 'What is it?'

Tom didn't say anything; he just glared in horror glancing around nervously at the strange small, black, prism-shaped volcanoes protruding out of the grey arid marshland. 'James! Morkann is here, I can feel it…'

James became silent, pensively scouring the parched, thirsty land although his eyes shot open wide like a raccoon in the night; he was too engrossed in watching where he would put his feet. James suddenly appeared with a dangerous stillness about him with deep fear etched upon his face. He glanced around the soggy marshland landscape for any sense of a direction. He knew he was the older brother and felt he would have to take charge of his younger sibling in this strange obscure land.

Suddenly, out of the silence, there was a loud, violent, roar. The terrain rocked and the stars fell, whatever it was. It was angry. As both boys glared in horror, the wrath was beginning to take form. The marshland beneath their feet quivered and shook. James held onto the hoop with feathers he had found earlier, grabbing Tom's arm to guide him.

Tom looked up at James with a reassuring smile, 'Here.' Tom handed James the sword by the gilded hilt. 'Take it, you may need this here.'

Taking the sword quickly, James grimaced and questioned, 'And you? What do you have?' He was referring to any weapons that Tom may have had and also to reassure himself that Tom was safe.

'Quickly take it, I have the…'

The Valley of Tongues

Just as Tom was about to tell James that he had the magic powder, which Jambalee had given him together with the shield of life, a bellowing roar sounded and everything shuddered again.

'What the—?' growled James. Tom quickly ducked, and James grabbed Tom, pulling him to the ground to hide behind an odd-shaped boulder.

The worried boys gawked at each other and gasped in trepidation whilst holding their breath. It was as if their nightmare had come true. Morkann's ghouls suddenly appeared hovering and wailing around the boys.

Their chant was deafening and sadistic. The rattling seemed to grow louder and louder, stronger and more vibrant like that of African drums playing hard, their vibrant chains clanking in the galactic space sounded like an irregular string orchestra.

'Where is that noise coming from?' asked James wearily, placing his hands onto his ears so as to protect them from the screeching sound. Staring at the strange surroundings in bewilderment, James glanced at Tom looking for an answer to his distress.

'It's her and her companions,' snapped a fearful Tom.

'You know, Jambalee once told me, "The sounds indicate that Morkann is near by and her Ghouls are seeking revenge." Do you remember the code, James?'

'If your enemy is hungry, feed him,
If he is thirsty...
give him something to drink...'

As Tom went on to continue speaking, James cut in and began to recite the scripture. In unison, they continued.

The Dream Catcher

*'In doing this,
you will heap burning coals
on his head.'*

'Yeah, yeah I know that. Isn't that's from the Good over Evil?'

'Yes it is. Come on—,' Tom snapped sharply at James.

'Okay, so how is that going to help us?' exclaimed James.

'James, I think Morkann's power will fade,–If she hears anything 'good' I mean the right scripture-that is!' Tom said persuasively.

As both boys held their weapons tightly and stood up from hiding behind the rock, they felt bolder, stronger, and ready for whatever they would confront.

Suddenly a bright light flashed by as both boys gazed up straight into the cold, dark atmosphere shadowed by the twinkling of stars and planets. Their eyes followed the bright flash of light zipping past.

'Wow! Did you see that?' asked Tom.

'I think that is the Lost Moon's visit to an intellectual cove, and it's on its way now to fuel the fires of the five-planet cluster in independent Arum!' stated a confident Tom.

James again looked on, convinced it was the light of Hakeem. 'Tom, is that—?' James snapped incredulously. 'It's Hakeem I am sure!'

Tom nodded and understood that Morkann's Ghouls were nearby.

Both boys had now started their arduous journey once again still watching their backs for either Jambalee or Hakeem. The noise became louder and louder, James turned to Tom.

'What is that muttering noise?' questioned an anxious James, listening intently to the incoherent sounds.

The Valley of Tongues

Tom, frowning in his brow and concentrating with a steely expression, glanced slowly around the arid terrain; he then patted his jacket pocket to make sure the powder was safely in his pocket. Stepping precariously on each rock on the lustrous grain, trying desperately not to slip, feeling the silver quicksand ground beneath his feet too inviting, Tom and James now began to take gentle giant steps trying to avoid the hazardous quicksand curdling and beckoning them. Both the boys were now able to hear clearly illogical sounds and incoherent noises. This was the language of Tongue. Both boys looked at each other in horror.

Tom glared back at his brother, petrified. He repeated word by word slowly. 'I think, James, we are in The Valley of Tongues, so I am assuming this muttering noise that we can hear is the language of Tongue!' stated Tom independently.

'...And this is what they speak—right?' continued an ever-inquisitive James, displaying a nervous smile to Tom.

Tom listened intently to the muttering, trying to translate the sound. "I can't make it out. What they are mumbling?' asked Tom. 'Can you try and figure the sounds out? I don't think it's Latin.'

James stopped suddenly, peering at a bowing old oak tree. It was large and seemed angry; its thick, leviathan trunk appeared to twist into the arid terrain with its distorted branches all barren and grey matted together to fall in front James. James looked intently at the tree, and then he glanced up at the shooting red comet in the dark horizon. James abruptly stopped pausing for a split second. He forgot about the muttering noise and that Morkann's Ghouls were now closer than ever.

'What on earth is going on here?' bellowed a confused James. He was now frowning in despair, caught up in a land of the unknown. He gawked on, intently watching the impact of strange

The Dream Catcher

characters appearing. They were in large crowds, made up of a mixture of Lupans and Dillyans with a few U-tags gathering as the grand pillar prominently gracing the terrain shook and shuddered. The grand pillar shook, as the tremor took hold as the boys heard loud noises, and then there was a terrible bang. Grey, hazy smoke emitted into the saffron coloured cosmic air space with light flashes of stares firing; James looked, his eyes open wide in bewilderment, watching in amazement.

The two boys slowly crept into the dense terrain, petrified of their quest. It was now clear whom they had been set out to seek— Hakeem and Princess Anna-Lisa were no-where to be seen, let alone Jambalee and Halaconia. They were now alone. All they could hear were the eerie sounds of open death and strange creatures. Tom gave James a steely stare and beckoned him to walk closer. The terrain was rugged and rough with obscure golden-red flames spewing out of floating comets, and as they looked at each flame like a ray of hope, it would stay for a fleeting moment and then wither into a ghost-like shape, twisting and swirling into an inviting hologram like that of an angel. But it wasn't an angel, and it suddenly went out, disappearing only to leave behind a silhouette of hope.

As they approached the edge of the terrain, they were able to view the cold, dark, rugged mountains of Moon. Suddenly it split into a labyrinth.

'Now what?' a puzzled James queried.

The boys did not know how to leave the maze. Something had gone wrong. Which way was going to lead them? James wondered. He peered into the vast space above, only being able to view shooting comets and light flashes in a deep void that was before him. He could now see the danger that lay before both of them.

The Valley of Tongues

It was a long narrow gauge, with a drop so piercing that there was no end to be seen. The smoke from the fountain was so treacherous that even the beings who lived on this land would never dare venture into this part of the Land of Tongues. The ravine fell to a sudden, horrendous, sheer death drop, as if it were to beckon Hell! Splashes of thick, silver, mercury-like liquid sprang out like silver dust and roared around the terrain causing grey, smouldering smoke to engulf the air.

The waves roared violently and slashed at the rocks as angry tyrants of mercury-type-liquid-filled shapes splashed and slapped on the mountainous rocks in front of him.

They clung onto each other as they slowly plodded on through the strange purple mulch ground. The sludgy, soggy terrain squashed under their feet as they slowly treaded each step precariously. James glanced up defiantly as he saw a strange tree which resembled a tongue.

'Errh…look at that, Tom. It's disgusting!' he moaned as he continued pacing through the purple mulch. The Tongue tree then quickly wrapped its pale crimson potted bark, resembling a long tongue, around another Tongue tree, pushing it to slide and follow the boys.

James gasped horrified. 'Look, Tom. That is awful, you know, I think we are being followed!' James moaned.

Tom turned around and witnessed a group of tongues following them. 'Oh my goodness! Look at this James… Look! Tom stammered turning James around to see the group of walking tongues. Clutching James and walking steadily but slowly, he asked, 'Now what…what do they want? Do you think they are hungry?' Tom yelped'

'I don't know!' James replied wearily.

The Dream Catcher

Just when the two boys thought they had reached their final destination James took a heavy sigh. James stared at Tom holding his head in his hands in despair. Tom guessed that James was in search for Princess Anna-Lisa and Hakeem, the tall character which appeared as an innocuous redwood tree. That was the arm, the light that had brought them both to the galaxy. Tom leant over to console his brother. They quickly turned after hearing some rustling, and as they both looked up in dismay, small meteorites fell. The boys were startled, still staring up into the dark, black sky containing the diamond, twinkling, star lights of the cosmos before them. Then, James could see a small head and part of a silver wing.

James nudged Tom. 'Look, what do think?' He asked anxiously. 'Do you think it could be...?' There was as pause as Tom peered intently petrified as to whom it would reveal.

James hoped it would be Halaconia. He wondered and hoped if the little green creature Jambalee was with her, too. He was right, and both James and Tom were elated as they saw what they had both waited to see. James and Tom ran as much as they could and as quick as they could. A waterlogged, teary-eyed Tom was euphoric. He knew that the loyal servant, Jambalee was back and they now would be guided away from danger. Halaconia was back, and she was not alone. James, too, sighed with a sense of relief. Along with her was the head of the Lupan army, Aspero, her betrothed one. They were going to assist both boys in their quest and together with Jambalee, the boys, and the army of brave, strong Lupans.

Jambalee smiled in jubilation, and Tom beamed a smile as wide as an ocean, elated and reassured that Jambalee would now surely assist with the rescue of Princess Anna-Lisa. He was now reassured that no matter what they did, Jambalee was sure to help.

The Valley of Tongues

A teary-eyed Tom hugged Jambalee with a longing embrace as James looked on. Jambalee returned the embrace giving a warm smile. Halaconia glanced at James and James at her but did not embrace. He was too embarrassed and felt she knew of his feelings for her. The awkward moment was also felt by Aspero. The strong, fearless leader of the army of Lupans was watching closely, and he knew there could never be true love but only affection between Halaconia, a creature with hooves, and a human, James if there was anything.

Jambalee released Tom from his embrace, holding him by his arms. The strong creature appeared worried. A teary-eyed Tom glared back, frowning in dismay.

'What is it? What has happened?' he asked inquisitively and troubled. Taking two steps back he turned to face Halaconia. James, by this time, had rushed to Tom's side. Frowning, he tried to console his brother not fully understanding what had happened.

'It is Princess Lindiarna, your mother. The wicked Morkann has taken her revenge with her Ghouls. The sound you hear now is the joyful chant from the Ghouls.'

Tom grimaced and frowned deeply and became very upset.

James cut in, 'Is my mum okay? Shall we go back home? So what are we going to do now?' he shouted.

The strong, powerful Aspero watched the two boys and saw the sorrow in the eyes of each child. He knew what was happening, so he blurted, 'I am sure Hakeem will be at the Oracle, and he will help you. You must save your mother first she is our true Queen!'

Tom knew that Linda was Princess Lindiarna but James did not, and he looked on with furrowed brow trying to match things up in his head, trying to establish how he had entered the world in which a strange character was now telling him that his mother,

The Dream Catcher

who shopped at the local supermarket, was a princess from a far-off land. It didn't seem to any make sense.

Aspero bellowed domineeringly, turning to his strong army who was brandishing swords with armoury wrapped around their strange bodies. Their white horses were strong and almost appeared to be intangible, ghostlike, muscular creatures. Their long manes flowed like wafts of feathers holding their power.

Tom and James were glued intently to hearing Aspero lecture his army. Both boys, now frowning, were concerned about how they would be able to rescue their mother. Alarmed and frightened, they listened to every word which was spoken. It was in Latin, so Tom nudged James to make sure he heard every word.

'Nos must vado dilgenter ut oust Morkann, suus exercitus est near,I mos tribuo signum?' Aspero bellowed.

James turned towards Tom robotically. He slowly reiterated in English as Aspero finished off his sentence, 'Tom, we are going *Nos must vado dilgenter ut oust Morkann, suus exercitus est near,I mos tribuo signum* to find her!'

His eyes open wide in fear, Tom turned sharply to face James. 'Who?' Tom yelped.

James continued whispering, 'Morkann!'

'That's what he said. Gosh, where is Hakeem and where has Jambalee gone?'

'We must go carefully to oust Morkann. Her army of ghouls are near. I will give the signal,' Aspero said, warning the boys of their plight.

As the army collected their weaponry and horses, Jambalee appeared, smiling. He turned to a worried James. 'Remember, there

The Valley of Tongues

is calm you can find when you dive deep beneath the rough waters on the surface James. Remember this.'

And with that he smiled at Tom continuing, 'Use your shield, Tom...use your shield.

'This is the same advice Hakeem gave you, do you remember?' suggested a thoughtful Aspero.

The army of Lupans chanted as they led the way, trudging in unison through the deep blue mist of vegetation soaked in mercury. There was a dank, decomposing stench around the atmosphere as if death were near. Both boys became anxious, and their faces were tired, and their bodies ached as they followed without causing any exertion. The army was proudly marching, brandishing their swords and shields. In their desperate display of strength they followed subserviently.

James continuously patted his jacket pocket to verify his hoop was still intact and in his pocket. He had no idea how important this hoop was, only that it was given to him by Hakeem and he had realised it had some power. It felt like hours had passed as the boys marched on unsure as to when their journey would end.

Suddenly they entered an area of black, damp, solemn darkness with a blue-grey mist haze hovering above in the atmosphere. There were no comets, no stars, no lost planets, no beings, no light, and no sense of happiness—just a chasm of darkness and strange, eerie noises.

It blended into a ghostlike eerie world, only small, open craters burbling on the ground. Both boys now marched on slowly, their hearts racing as their sweat dripped in anxiety. Then they heard a slap of feet on the ground. It was a dull sound, and it was near and becoming closer and louder. Both boys looked up sharply, turning

The Dream Catcher

to each other. James suddenly turned around to see a shadowy figure glaring at both boys. He could hear the slap of feet on the ground closing in behind them.

He turned to face Tom. Tom screamed, hoping the army would hear him, but the army did not hear the shriek. Aspero's army had trudged on ahead and were now a long distance away. They could see shadows of carcasses dying. The battlefield went dark—only sounds told a story of sadness and despair.

James could hear a vibration of screams then sudden loud anger. Tom looked on; he could only see light appear for a second then it would disappear just as quick only reappearing for a flicker of a moment. Tom and James increased their speed until they were running as fast as they could. Behind them they could clearly hear a babbling chorus of the pursuit. A shadow of a bony, spindly hand snatched at Tom's shoulder. He could feel the touching of the emaciated fingers digging deep in to his child-like body. Screaming and squealing, he tried to twist away from the clasp. As he did so he could feel that the figure had split his jacket causing it fall over his shoulder. Tom, now blind in terror, stumbled as he looked up at James, shaking in disbelief.

Taking in a deep breath, he stammered, 'That...that was her—MORKANN!' Tom paused trying to complete each word. He was scared stiff.

James, realising Morkann's pursuit, comforted Tom. Frowning and looking up at the atmosphere, he shouted in Latin then in English *'Licentia nos unus! Leave us alone!'*

Both boys began to plod on through the terrain, trudging on the marshland and still hearing the eerie echo howling around them. As both boys walked on, a red smog engulfed them, suddenly swallowing up the atmosphere. James felt a heavy wave of a figure

The Valley of Tongues

fleeting past him, but he could not see, for he was blinded by the dense smog in front. He stumbled. As he tried to raise himself up he was struck again, and suddenly he could feel the heat from the red smog becoming intense on his face and through his thin clothing. James tried to call out to Tom, but Tom could not hear as he had become deaf for that split second.

The misty dense smog had taken hold of their senses, and the Ghouls were laughing malevolently around them. Unexpectedly, James felt a burst of agony paralysing his legs. He was unable to raise them, and he dropped to his knees like a pack of cards.

Unable to continue and in sheer despair he grimaced at his anguish. 'Argh! Tom! Where are you? I can't walk!' he moaned.

Tom fumbled his way through the misty, dense smog and found James. He tried to help James up but was unable to.

Then Morkann's Ghouls began to rein them in. Both boys looked at each other, petrified and frightened at their fate. A palisade of strange bodies and gloating, blood-crazed faces scared and mocked. Out of their wide eyes oozed blood that dripped in harmony accompanied by an evil chant. All of a sudden there was a pause in their harmonious evil welcome rant; Morkann had entered the Valley of Tongues.

James was in agony trying to hold his legs, glaring down at James with a steely stare she spoke, 'You are the brave one! James, I know you have come to rescue the princess!' She bellowed in Latin, *'Vos es fortis unus! James EGO teneo vos adeo eripio Procer!'*

Tom stared back at Morkann, fixated on her venomous strands of hair with the snakes slithering and sliding through her tresses of black and green snake hair. As she spoke, her deep and hollow, green emerald eyes sank into a spellbinding trance. Tom tried desperately not to look at her penetrating eyes.

The Dream Catcher

'Gaze, dear boy. Gaze at me!' She laughed a menacing scream, howling whilst letting out a perilous shriek.

Tantalizingly she glared at James, knowing he had spoken Latin.

'So *Vos reputo vos can iuguolo mihi? Operor vos? Ha! Ha! You think you can kill me?* Do you? How wrong you are!' she sneered, laughing away.

The Ghouls wailed and swished in the air, laughing a menacing groan, a hoarse, sensual laughter, crowding the boy, jostling around him as if a blood-thirsty sport was being played. James was petrified; sweat trickled down his face, and his eyes became waterlogged. Then with a wild yell, he had a sudden brain wave. He thought of his hoop and ever so carefully pulled it out of his pocket so as not to be seen. The Ghouls hollowed around him, sensing something was being carried out. James held onto his hoop tightly. He now had the hoop in his hand. Tom could now see how James was trying to hide the hoop from Morkann's gaze and away from the Ghouls.

The Ghouls were dangling Tom from his ankles, taunting him, wailing and hissing and jostling him through the air. These strange creatures frightened Tom with their menacing faces and their deafening noises, piercing his ears; he raised both his arms to cover his now-squeezed face fighting back his tears of horror. Tom was now hanging like a rag doll. As the Morages held him loosely from his ankles, Tom clung onto his life, groaning and shouting to James to use anything to rescue him.

Out of the blue Morkann appeared and then lashed out at the boy, her long black cloak dragging on the ground. Her long, scrawny fingers reached for his neck. Each bone was visible, and her fingernails were pointed and sharp as a dagger. Tom watched in horror, he shuddered, he could see James trying hard to hide the hoop from Morkann's gaze as he tried to inconspicuously use

The Valley of Tongues

the hoop to save him from the taunt. He knew James would find that apt moment to wave the hoop and dispel the evil around him at a precise second. Both boys were waiting in terror when out of the blue, there was a flash of white, bright, dazzling light. It was Hakeem who appeared. James was relieved, and Tom let out a moan as he held back his tears.

'Let me go!' Tom shouted defiantly to the Morages still holding him tightly by his ankles as Morkann fluttered away trying to hide from Hakeem.

'Let him go!' she raged.

James was holding the hoop tightly in his hand. He could now see how Hakeem had thundered through in a rupture of light. Morkann flew across the air to scurry away from the tall carrier of good. It was obvious that she was unable to display her wrath in his presence. Her Ghouls still dangling Tom from his ankles released him, hastily hoping he would fall to his death.

Tom screamed, 'Argh...arggggh!'

Hakeem caught him in his muscular hands. He then placed him carefully onto the ground; he turned and roared at the army of ranting Ghouls. At that moment the Ghouls whimpered away and followed Morkann, wafting their muslin, grey-white gowns through the air with their sullen, morose, drooping, open, bloodthirsty mouths revealing hollow voids of hell.

Hakeem had rescued the boys.

James gazed onto his hands and Tom grabbed his Hakeem's thumb. They could feel the warmth of his hand and comfort. A white smog covered them and then dwindled away. It had all but disintegrated into the distance, and Tom was still sniffling in pain from his ankles as he looked up at the towering creature.

The Dream Catcher

'Hell...hello. Thanks,' he said, wiping his nose on his sleeve.

James, peering up at a strange but helpful character, wondered if he had left the hoop behind or whether it was Hakeem who had left the Dream Catcher hoop for him to take. Still in deep thought, he pondered and plucked up the courage to ask.

'Did you leave me this for me?' he asked, dangling the Dream Catcher to him.

Hakeem glanced quickly at the hoop and paused taking a gulp of air. 'You must be careful. It is there for your dream. Just make sure Xle-Ha does not get hold of it.'

'Xle-Ha? Who is that?' James queried, puzzled as he had never heard of the strange name before.

Tom was still nursing his sore ankles and trying to stop the blood from oozing out. Whilst still continuing to sniffle, he gave a steely stare to James and then said, 'James, I know. I think he is the one who lives on the Mountains of Moon. I think he was the one Jambalee told me to make sure he did not get hold of that hoop! Am I right, Hakeem?'

Hakeem did not speak, but he stretched out his giant-like palm. In it was the flickering of a flame a star—Hayley's Star.

Then a loud deep voice reverberated. 'I am Hakeem, bearer of all that is good. I carry Hayley's Star and the light of lost dreams. You are a good person, and I know your dream, James! Do you remember what Jambalee told you?'

James turned to try and stare with a determined look at the overbearing being and with a deep frown froze. He then turned to face Tom, who was still busy nursing his saw-cut ankles trying to stop his thick blood from seeping out. James was in turmoil not fully understanding why this creature had become their friend,

The Valley of Tongues

when suddenly the boys had a spark, a brain wave. They looked at each other, both remembering in verbatim which word had been said, when cautiously they smiled collectively.

They then repeated each word slowly in unison, *'Remember, there is calm you must find when you dive deep beneath the rough waters on the surface you must remember this!'*

James paused and stopped, relieved that he was able to remember what the huge being had said before. He was now wide-eyed in anxiety, and with a deep frown he interrupted abruptly, 'Yes, I remember.' He paused still thinking. 'But what SURFACE are you talking about and who is Xle-Ha?' He looked perplexed.

Hakeem pointed to Aspero and his army in the distance. Again he spoke in a deep, loud, penetrating voice which reverberated through the horizon bouncing off from each mountain and comet. 'I will take you to Aspero and his army of Lupans. Jambalee will meet you at the site of the Oracle. Jambalee will make sure Xle-ha does not reach the Dream Catcher.'

Then Hakeem stretched out his long arm towards the boys. It was still draped in a white robe, covered in foliage which seemed to merge with the light beaming through. He opened his thick, muscular hand displaying his colossal palm laden with deep lines. 'James, look after the Dream Catcher. You will need this!' Hakeem bellowed to James.

Both boys grimaced to each other as they cautiously climbed aboard. Then suddenly with a great boom a fireball erupted in a rage of red and orange fire flames. James grabbed Tom by his hand. The sixteen-year old child had now become a man. He had to rescue his mother, look after his younger sibling Tom, and take charge of the battle with Morkann.

The Dream Catcher

Hakeem glided into the deep, dark galaxy illuminated only by the stars and comets dazzling around. Bewildered, James's and Tom's faces lit up. They curled their faces, protecting them from the sharp rays of fire. A large plume of black smoke erupted and from its smog King Polyectes, King of Moriadiya, Morkann's evil father, appeared alive. He let out a bewitching laugh.

Tom recognised him immediately as James shouted abruptly, 'Oh Goodness, who is he? Give me the sword, Tom. Quick!' James was enraged by this powerful confrontational creature.

James again shrieked, hoping Tom would throw him the sword.

Tom quickly threw the gilded heavy sword still in its hilt over to James. 'Catch it!'

Then Tom with a forlorn face still petrified for James's safety, pulled out of his pocket the magic white powder. Whilst throwing the sword towards James, he knew this magic powder—if anything—would work.

Tom shouted to James throwing the jewel-laden sword to him. James caught it with a cold, sharp, steely stare and his eyes wide open. The sword shimmered and each jewel began to lift. Hakeem thundered across the ground so as to protect the boys.

King Polyectes roared in terror, 'You don't scare me! I should have killed King Cepheus when I had the chance!'

He let out a menacing shriek echoing around him. He yelled, throwing his chains around, and as he paced, his voice reverberated and bounced off from the comets and each rock strewn across the tor.

Aspero, who was seated on a strong, white, muscular Unicorn turned to Halaconia. Hearing the muted noises of voices bouncing off from the rocks, he turned sharply and saw the boys with Hakeem in dispute with King Polyectes. Halaconia then silently

The Valley of Tongues

looked at Aspero hoping he would command and give the orders to his army to quickly rescue Tom and James. Halaconia, not waiting for a reply, was now becoming anxious. She frowned and lifted her silver, transparent wings, and with a quick burst of energy she flew in to the distance to check on the boys.

Aspero turned to his beloved sleek Unicorns; he watched them adoringly and cherished their graceful movements. They bowed subserviently and gracefully glided into the air.

'Go and rescue all that is good my loyal friends!' Aspero said.

He knew the battle which he had dreaded had begun, and he knew of the horrors Morkann and King Polyectes were capable of undertaking. Aspero realised that many of his loyal Lupans and Centaurs would die or be killed. He frowned in a deep sorrow, taking in a deep gulp of air and biting his bottom lip so as to hold out his square jaw. But he realised there was no choice. And as a leader he would have to show courage allowing his army and Unicorns to die.

Halaconia turned to her betrothed Aspero. "You will make the right decision,' she said and smiled reassuringly at him. She fluttered away with her silver, translucent wings again into the distance.

Aspero roared, commanding his sleek, white, muscular, winged army of graceful Unicorns whilst gently stroking and admiring his fleet. He bowed his head and then instructed the Wish Unicorn to lead. The Unicorns displayed their graceful, toned, and slender bodies with silky, white hides along with their silver, dazzling horns emulating rays of a night's prism. They bowed their heads, fluttering their long black eyelashes and turned rigidly to face the battle with King Polyectes and his army of Munch-faced Moorags.

James watched the strange, powerful King intently. His long, black, wiry hair swiped the floor covering his eerie sullen face.

The Dream Catcher

His glass-white, diamond eyes menacingly glared as he frowned at James, his ranting anger at Hakeem and Tom. His rage shuddered through the galactic air space. James then flexed his neck and looked closely at the strange surrounding glaring at King Polyectes in terror. The small red comets dispersed in a fountain of beams sending light flashes through the cosmic atmosphere. Tom took in a deep breath and looked on with a forlorn glare hesitating as to whether he should speak or not.

He glanced over at the immensely large, towering Hakeem and then quickly down at James, who appeared by contrast to be a quivering ant. He gradually opened his mouth trying to mime, indicating to James he should use the magic powder—anything to help—but he stopped, hesitating for a moment and then continued again. Tom slowly tried to speak, pausing each time in fear; he stopped for a second then rubbed his head in anguish. 'How am I going to get his attention?' he questioned to himself.

Tom turned towards Hakeem, and in deep trepidation held out his shaking, clammy hand, trying to touch Hakeem's arm, which in contrast felt tough, hard, and dense like a thick block of cold iron. Tom tried to raise his head to look up to Hakeem, but he was too tall. He could only see sunlight beaming back down into his eyes, blinding him; he had to find a way, any small way he could to tell him that James was in danger, but then Hakeem could see anything. He saw everything—surely he would know. After all, he was the powerful one.

Tom quickly glanced back over at James who was watching King Polyectes with his army of Moorags now howling like banshees with their open, blood-thirsty, sullen, long mouths drooping wide, clearly scaling the area around James for a fresh new kill. James

The Valley of Tongues

knew he had to get back to Tom, and Tom knew he had to rescue James—but how?

He was now surrounded by wailing Moorags, each glaring at their fresh kill. They were ready; they swished and swirled in their drapery and with their tight piercing ice-blue eyes, ripped through the core of James's heart. He went cold and shuddered; his hands were shaking as sweat trickled down his forehead like rivulets in a fountain and then gradually dripped onto his shoulder drip by drip, falling like icicles and then suddenly evaporating on to his torso.

Tom nervously shouted at James, stepping back into the thick marshland. 'James, you have to get that Dream Catcher ring out of your pocket now! Just do it,' Tom screamed at the top of his voice frowning in anxiety.

James quickly gazed towards Tom, who now was frantic and frightened at the wailing of Moorags crowding him. James, wide-eyed, started to pull at his pockets desperately trying to yank out the strange hoop with feathers which Tom had referred to. The noise was intense and very loud, vibrating violently all around him in a droning clamour. Echoing around the galaxy, bouncing off from the fallen golden stars, yet no-one could help. James was the only one able to hear, out of all the confusion around them, the strange clatter suddenly became muffled, except for the wailing of malicious Moorags. James was in despair and felt completely uneasy and for the first time fearful for his life. Tom licked his lips in anticipation, hoping, his heart racing fast and beating like a drum thumping louder and louder. He was praying they would be saved or at least be able to disappear.

Tom just wanted everything to swallow him up and for him to wake up as if it were a dream. He tried to think about the tools he was carrying: the sword, the Dream Catcher ring, and the powder. Which one of them would work? He thought about how he so

The Dream Catcher

longed for his friend Jambalee to be present. As he closed his eyes for that split-second, which felt like a year, he let a single tear drop and called to his mum. Momentarily his conscience beckoned his mother.

His prayers had been answered. Jambalee appeared. Tom gleamed and beamed an open-wide smile, happy and relieved to see his loyal friend. Tom knew he and his brother would now be rescued and saved.

Jambalee hugged Tom and gave a half smile for he knew there was not much time and they were all in danger. James threw the hoop towards King Polyectes and watched intently as it shimmered in a golden glow bubble. Jambalee peered over at the light whilst holding Tom away to protect his eyes and him.

"Guard your eyes, Tom', he hollered, taking the gilded sword in his hand from the heavy jewelled hilt.

"James, look out, duck! The Unicorns, Centaurs—they have all returned now to help us, look!"

Jambalee pointed to the rush of creatures who were trying to assist in the battle with King Polyectes. They roared past in a tumultuous stampede. Jambalee was glad he had returned to help the boys. He reminisced on the kindness of King Cepheus and how he had done so much for the galaxy. He owed this to his Princess Lindiarna, the real Queen as well as Queen to her boys Tom and James.

The army of Unicorns raged through towards the screeching Moorags as they swayed and fluttered across the tor. They galloped through the meanders to reach the ravine proudly. This soon became a fatal mistake. From the entrance of the galaxy a cloud mist lifted, gradually allowing the seeping of dull patches of purple light glowing far beyond the cosmic meteoroids floating around. The Morages lured each Unicorn, slowly wailing, fluttering, beckoning

The Valley of Tongues

each one in trickery into their death. The beautiful graceful Unicorns fell like pebbles into an inviting, deep, black ocean.

Tom and James watched in horror as each beautiful creature plunged to his death. The sound of death was dense and muted with a deep droning noise. They could see how the Moorags blended ghostlike into the precipitation-soaked terrain and how they would then let out a deafening screech fleeting into the distance. As each Unicorn appeared, displaying their sleek, graceful, silver horns they seemed to float, unreal intangible, almost magical. Each Unicorn galloped in the hope they could make a difference. They were helping Aspero; they were righteous. Their silver-white hide and toned muscles displayed their agility but that was all in vain, for they were unaware of what was before them. The Moorags lured each creature to their pointless death at the lip of the crater, beckoning the helpless creature to its innocent death. James tried in vain to persuade the Unicorns not to go further into the ditch by shouting and waving his arms around like some insane creature. But it was to no avail, and then suddenly he was pulled back by Jambalee who was worried that he too may be attacked. James anxiously pulled out the hoop from his pocket. He held the Dream Catcher hoop high and saw it flash for a split second. He wishfully prayed, but nothing happened. He repeated it again as sweat trickled in rivulets down his face and onto his shoulders. He was tired and turned to Tom. With a turned-up lip, he frowned in despair realising nothing was to save what was written. Both boys glared in horror as Jambalee gave a steely gaze at the slaughter.

As each Unicorn fell into the open crater a deep screech and moan was emitted and then a thunderbolt of light flashed suddenly fluttering into the horizon followed by the pungent smell of dead burning flesh.

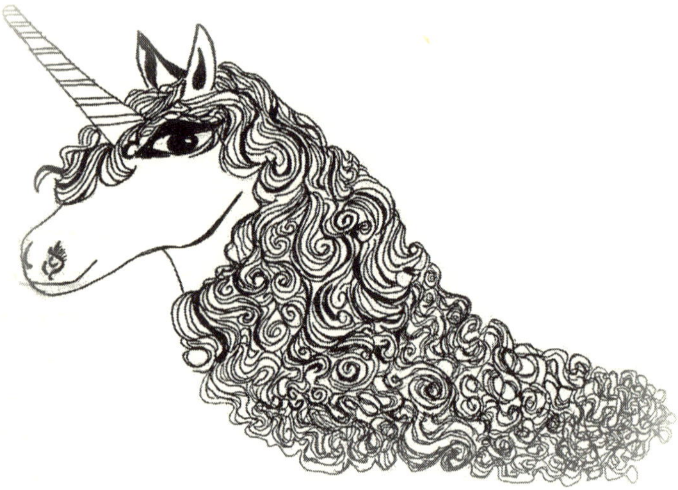

The Valley of Tongues

James watched helplessly. How could he help prohibit the slaughter? He looked on, pondering in deep thought, knowing what had happened.

'We have got to do something!' he yelled angrily.

'I know…but what?' Tom replied, fighting back his tears.

The lights of the carcasses died, the battlefield went dark, and what stars remained disappeared leaving behind a cold, callous breeze sending sharp shivers through the boy's marrow. Only muted, droning sounds remained, telling the story of a fight full of trickery and evil. King Polyectes had shown his wrath, and his army had carried out the evil deed.

Jambalee wearily looked at the boys. 'Come, we must go. There is nothing more we can do here,' he said in a deep melancholy voice, peering at the destruction of the Unicorns.

'But we have to try SOMETHING…we've got to rescue…we can't just let it…' James abruptly stopped short of his sentence; he glanced at the mayhem of that which had occurred. He paused. He could see a Unicorn gripping onto his life; he was struggling on the edge of the crater where he had fallen. He was taking deep breaths and then suddenly stopping, panting for air, then pausing. His graceful hide inflated then collapsed with each toned muscle stretching out as he struggled to breathe. There beside him lay carcasses of Unicorns all groaning in pain strewn across the strange naked rock of the crater. Those creatures that had died and withered away lay still as stone with their silver horns disintegrating into silver dust. But not this one. He was a fighter. There was something unique about this one, something magical.

The Unicorn gazed at James with his big, wide-open eyes fluttering, his long eyelashes in despair, and James then quickly realised he had to be rescued somehow. But how? He scratched his

The Dream Catcher

forehead and glimpsed over at Jambalee and Tom whilst precariously walking into the ditch.

James rushed over towards the unicorn as both Jambalee and Tom looked on helplessly. James jumped into the ridge of the crater so that he was able to hold the creature. He stroked his sleek, slender neck; he could see fear looming in the Unicorn's wide, sad, sapphire eyes as he grimaced in pain, trying not to cry out. His breathing was laboured and slow. James comforted the Unicorn as much as he could. Tearfully kneeling, he grabbed at Tom's trouser leg as he was standing nearby tying to pull out the pot containing the white magic powder.

'Tom, give me that powder!'

Tom handed the magic powder pot hurriedly, hoping to rescue the creature. Jambalee held Tom's hand.

'James, you be careful!' shouted Jambalee, concerned for his safety.

Jambalee and Tom watched carefully as James tried to place small drops into the Unicorn's mouth.

'Open your mouth…please, come on! Please open your mouth…we're gonna help you…please take it…come on,' he said sorrowfully, trying to suppress his tears.

He struggled, trying to desperately prize open the creature's strong jaw in order to place the magic powder drops into the Unicorn's mouth. Slowly he succeeded; grabbing the creature's strong jaw with one hand, he dropped a couple of the powder droplets into its mouth.

The Unicorn could not swallow so easily and blinked his teary, large, pear-shaped, sapphire eyes. Painfully he gulped the powder down. Tom watched wide-eyed like a hooting owl in amazement.

The Valley of Tongues

James gratefully caressed the animal as it appeared the powder had worked.

'They were all trying to help us! It's okay,' he said, trying to comfort the struggling creature. He waited for the creature to move further but he did not. James caressed the Unicorn again fighting back his tears. He felt the Unicorn had survived, but he wasn't moving.

Jambalee hovered precariously over towards James and placed his hand on his shoulder. He knew that that the Unicorn was dying. After a brief silence Jambalee glanced over at Tom who was also sobbing in the distance; he beckoned him to approach his brother and to go and leave the creature to his fate.

'You have done what is right, James…Come on, we must go now—there is nothing more you can do for him,' Tom said tearfully with a forlorn look on his face.

James looked up at Tom with a steely stare and with waterlogged eyes. And holding back his tears defiantly he questioned, 'You said this stuff worked!' He held up the powder pot towards Tom and Jambalee. 'Hakeem said, do you remember, there is a calm you can find when you dive deep beneath the rough waters on the surface? Do you remember…Tom? DO YOU REMEMBER?'

He bellowed angrily as he watched the Unicorn slowly suffer. James looked at the silver-white Unicorn lying in the crater, sweat streaming down its face in rivulets as the Unicorn grimaced in pain, trying not to cry out, but James could see and feel the fear looming in its large melancholy, sapphire eyes. James stroked and caressed the injured creature. Feeling the prickly small hairs from his hide flatten together to form a warm, sleek coat against his skin as their

The Dream Catcher

bodies started to meld together James felt he had to do something for this creature that seemed to defy all odds.

'We can't help him—James, it's too late!' Jambalee said.

James turned sharply and glared up at the purple misty sky, listening to the cries and wailing sounds of Morkann's Ghouls battling in the distance with the Centaurs and Aspero with his army of Lupans. Their cries reverberated around the atmosphere like an operatic séance.

Still sniffling and caressing the unicorn James turned to Tom, 'Something has gone wrong, Tom!' James frowned and dipped his head in sorrow, and with a forlorn steely stare he said, 'Didn't your powder work before?'

Tom hesitated, licking his lips, and took a deep sigh, pausing defiantly not knowing how to answer his older brother. Jambalee cut into an awkward silence as he turned back to see the Unicorn. As he watched he could see slight movement in the Unicorn's limbs.

'James, look!' He gasped. 'Quickly fetch some more powder—quick! You've done it, James, you've done it! You never gave up!'

James hurriedly ran back and jumped into the crater's ridge to the dying Unicorn handing over the drops from the pot containing powder to Jambalee. Jambalee then administered some more of the drops into his jaw watching very carefully the creature's movements.

'He's alive, James! You've done it!' Jambalee rejoiced. James was ecstatic.

Tom gave a sigh of relief that the Unicorn was saved. James let out a big smile and beamed a glow of happiness that the Unicorn had been rescued.

'Hey, it's working—it worked!' James stammered. He let out a wide smile and caressed the creature adoringly. Although he was one of many Unicorns that had come to assist in the battle and

The Valley of Tongues

many had died, this one had survived against all the odds. James felt compassion towards this extraordinary creature and was happy that he had rescued the Unicorn.

Suddenly a bright white light flashed back into his horn, and as it shimmered it caused a small diamond meteorite to float over the Unicorn and then away in to the red, hazy, cosmic horizon. The Unicorn's wide, pear-shaped, sapphire eyes dazzled like fresh-cut jewels as if they were immersed in a sparkling crystal sea; the Unicorn shimmered intently as life itself was born again. James and Tom gazed in awe and then turned quickly to face each other, both wide-eyed in bewilderment.

It was a success. They had rescued the Unicorn and brought him back to life. However, Tom knew it was all because of James that the Unicorn lived.

Jambalee approached the older sibling tenderly, and gently patted him on his shoulder. With a strong stare he turned to James. "Well done, my young one! You were right; it was only because of you and your tenacious spirit! Because of you, he will be okay, he will now live. Give him some more of the powder so he may walk with us on our journey. You were brave to make this decision alone; I applaud you, dear James. Now we must get him out of this ridge and take him on our journey.'

James smiled bashfully, dipping his head coyly; he was humble as he felt it was his duty. James had taken the advice of his mother, who had taught him about the Good Samaritan. And so he really didn't want any justification as to what he had done.

The two boys and Jambalee together with the now-healed, white, graceful unicorn set on their arduous journey through the barren marshland. Day after day the search continued. At last they came across a strange spectacular site of crimson and luscious green

The Dream Catcher

rich with foliage. It invited them all in to walk further and as they did so they could see in the faint distance a shadow of silver rippling silently gently.

James smiled. 'We are here!' he said to the others as he led them into Xle-Ha's trap.

Chapter IV
The Calm beneath the Surface

They all walked on pensively through the hazardous terrain. They could hear the faint moans and shrieks from the battle in the fading distance echoing in the galaxy, and at the same time each screech was heard a sudden burst of light was emitted. James turned to Tom in despair. Jambalee peered over at both the boys. He could sense their uneasiness.

Whilst peering at the boys, he questioned inquisitively, 'Come, we must locate the calm and find the deep beneath the rough waters of that surface. That's what he said?' Jambalee questioned assertively, trying to divert the boys' attention.

'So, where is this deep water then?' James retorted sharply as he rubbed his brow in anxiety.

'Come, I will lead you…you have the Dream Catcher—right?' Jambalee asked with a half smile whilst helping Tom carefully across the small crater on the ground.

James searched again, thrusting his hand into his jacket pocket just to make sure that the Dream Catcher hoop was with him. 'Yeah, got it!' James yelled excitedly, brandishing the strange hoop in his hand.

The Dream Catcher

'What about Aspero?' James asked with a slight tremble in his voice.

Tom gave James a steely gaze as if to suggest that he was asking a ridiculous question. Jambalee in turn gave an amorphous stare.

'Oh, Aspero is on your side. You don't need to worry about him. You need to worry about Xle-ha!' Jambalee gave a silent stare and walked towards Tom.

'Come Tom,' Jambalee said, pointing to Tom.

James quickly interrupted. 'Who is Xle-ha?' he asked in trepidation.

Jambalee gazed deeply at James and then with a reassuring smile said calmly, 'Xle-Ha is someone who wants the Dream Catcher, nothing else. He will do anything to get hold of it. He is from the Utargs, the clan who were dwarfed, but he has regained his strength and knows about the Dream Catcher. He wants to break out of his life here. James, we must make sure he does not get hold of it! Right; we just need to go a bit further.' Jambalee tried to encourage the boys to go further and to try and warn James from Xle-Ha. They had to get to where the calm was to be found below the surface.

Tom looked up at the misty, hazy, blue starlight which mingled with the sporadic dunes of rock and comets strewn across the sand-blasted ground. He then turned back to hear the sounds of the battle in the distance, which now sounded like sharp blasts of muted sirens. He could no longer hear the cries and screams that had painted a picture of a monotonous, slow death. He could only now hear a dull drone and slight insipid clatter of spears being shunt around. However, he was able to see a few bright white and green light flashes sporadically in the distance floating into a trance across the galactic air space displaying like a concord of fireworks in a wild explosion.

The Calm beneath the Surface

James nervously turned back, peering at his brother and at Jambalee. He shrugged his shoulders. With his eyes wide open and his eyebrows raised he questioned, 'So where is this water?'

Jambalee glanced back at both boys and lightly smiled, pointing to a ripple of silver glistening in a large bubble. Masterfully turning to the boys he said, 'Look! There it is. Carina's Drift and beneath that is the Calm!'

'But Jambalee, how will you get to the Calm? It's too far away and also THIS silver liquid does not look like a river!' Tom said, his lips tightly compressed.

James crinkled his eyes as he tried to get a good look at Carina's Drift and at Xle-Ha, who was still proudly standing with his chest prominent, displaying the writings of some ancient chant. James was in total awe as to this strange overbearing character.

The extreme heat from the flames sprayed onto his face, making it glow with rivulets of sweat. The intensity was sweltering, and James could feel the danger which lay ahead as he stood perplexed as to how he would even contemplate entering the liquid.

Jambalee gave Tom a hesitant chuckle. 'You're right. It is dangerous, and it is no ordinary river but we are going to have to find that calm. Right?' he said, holding his chest whilst holding his body and head erect. Jambalee gave the boys a straight gaze and squared up his small shoulders whilst clenching his fists. 'You will be alright; you have goodness on your side.'

He turned to the boys with a fearful frown. The rescued Unicorn became nervous, making a neighing sound of fear. He buckled and kicked not wishing to go any further and stopping midway before the ridge; James gently stroked his neck looking into the deep, gazelle-shaped, sad eyes of this mysterious creature.

The Dream Catcher

"What is it?' James asked the Unicorn as if expecting a reply. He caressed its long silver mane.

The Unicorn bowed its svelte neck and nudged at James in his stomach, trying to warn him not to go any further.

'Hey, it's okay. I am gonna be fine,' James said whilst he stroked his new friend.

Tom watched how a strong bond was now becoming apparent between James and the strange beast.

Tom looked at James and smiled endearingly at the Unicorn who was gradually now developing into their loyal friend in this strange galactic world.

'You know you are going to have to name him, don't you,' suggested Tom.

'I know,' replied a weary James stroking the unicorn.

Jambalee had always known that the stream of inviting liquid that seemed to resemble water was perilous and that the merciless Xle-Ha would be clad in his trade-mark animal kingdom big cat hide along with his distinctive, decorative, menacing markings on his chest displaying a ritual of death. He would almost certainly display his incandescent ash particles as he would emerge from the 'calm below the deep, hidden within Carina's Drift.' Those ash particles would surely disperse like a glowing cloud moving away from the Yellowstone magma at great speed and thus annihilating everything in its path.

Jambalee glared at James in terror. 'James, you will see him. He is fierce, but you are Lindiarna's son, the first-born son, and he will know of this.' Jambalee then gave James a reassuring smile and handed him the magic pot of powder.

'Take this. Remember—the goodness is with you.'

'Xle-Ha is, if you like, a shape-shifter, perhaps the best you will ever see.'

The Calm beneath the Surface

This stream was vigorous, and an optimistic silver-blue in colour. It shimmered its rays across its surface as if to beckon a jeweller to touch, if he would dare. In its core lived the untouchable Xle-Ha. Here he lived and here he slept, yet if disturbed he would destroy whomever would dare take its wrath.

He would wake up like a troll in a blaze and kill instantly with his raging power engulfing the territory like a hungry dog. However, Jambalee knew that he had no other choice and would have to take the risk for the boys to cross Carina's Drift and escape the wrath of Xle-Ha if they were to accomplish this endeavour and to reach the tower where Princess Anna-Lisa was held.

Precariously the boys stepped up further towards the Yellowstone magma which was filled with burning orange molten rock. It blazed and crackled in the intense smouldering heat. They watched it slowly cascade into a large crater creeping on the bottom of the mountain rock.

Aghast at where the boys had wondered, James blurted still holding his dear Unicorn, 'You can't go there!'

He was startled and shocked at the intensifying heat that was suddenly being generated.

Jambalee and Tom gazed at him and in unison retorted sharply, 'Why not? Come on, we are going to have to do this.' The Unicorn hesitated and buckled jerking away from the burning heat and rocks.

As he stopped, James realised the place he was about to enter was dangerous, very dangerous. He dipped his brow cautiously frowning, 'Are you sure about this?' He turned to Tom whilst comforting his Unicorn.

Jambalee peered at a nervous James. 'James you were the one who rescued the Unicorns. You are now going to rescue the princess. I know that you will succeed.'

The Dream Catcher

As the three of them and the Unicorn stepped up closer to the baseline of the silver floating liquid, their hearts began to pound. James became agitated, and he frowned. He could feel his hand become hot and clammy. Halaconia watched in the distance as she fluttered her transparent silver wings so as not to disturb their concentration. All three of them were walking tightly together, frightened into an abyss.

James glared with his eyes wide open and twinkling brightly in the gloom as to what they would expect when all of a sudden a bright white light from the floating stars slowly snapped, transforming into a dull grey mist. Suddenly it became pitch black. Eventually there was only nothing. No one could see anyone.

Tom grabbed James's arm. 'Are you here?' Tom asked nervously as he fondled his hands over what he felt was James's arm.

'Yeah! Get off me! Come on.'

Jambalee took the sword out of the jewelled hilt and held it high so that it glistened.

'You two boys okay?' asked a pensive Jambalee. 'I think, Tom, you may want to climb onto the Unicorn.'

James walked over to his white unicorn companion and stroked his slender coat, patting his neck. He turned to Tom.

'Climb on Tom,' said Jambalee, persuading James that it was okay to let go. 'They're good creatures; he will save you from Xle-Ha. I remember how I raised your mother Princess Lindiarna up as my own just as your Grandfather, King Cepheus, helped me!"

At that point, there was a sudden jerk, and the Unicorn sprang forward. It was almost as if the creature knew Tom was to ride him. Tom gripped tightly with his hands onto his silver mane. He bent his knees and crouched low over his silver-white, svelte, slender-toned body as Tom carefully rolled over onto the Unicorn's back.

The Calm beneath the Surface

He could feel the prickly hairs flatten together to form a warm, sleek coat against his skin as their bodies started to meld together.

They approached the ridge of the silver liquid.

Halaconia quickly fluttered past. 'Jambalee, where are you taking these boys?' she questioned strongly with her slender, silky arms holding her thin, svelte waist. Her translucent wings flapped together as they settled into position. Halaconia gazed around the sullen dark surroundings and then she noticed the Unicorn that had been rescued.

'Wow, you saved him?' she asked, joyfully hugging the creature. She then fluttered towards Jambalee who was sizing the dangerous silver river.

Jambalee knew he would have to cross the drift without disturbing Xle-Ha. Halaconia approached him anxiously, and in doing so she caught James eye.

He was looking at her in awe. 'You're back?' he said hoping for a conversation to begin.

James gazed up at the strange adorable creature with beautiful, burnished bonze hair draping her slender gazelle like-neck. He watched her silently caressing his Unicorn and smiling at Tom sitting on his Unicorn.

Halaconia smiled and then flew over to Jambalee who was busy looking at the silver sea intently. 'What are you doing?' she questioned.

'Ehmm, I have to see where this fire is strongest.'

'But, Jambalee, how will you get in there safely? It's seems too deep and dangerous. Isn't that sulphur water?, I am sure it will blow. You could awake Xle-Ha!'

'I know all the dangers, Halaconia. Those boys are of paramount importance. I just need to make sure that the powder I

The Dream Catcher

have given Tom and the Dream Catcher which James has will work, because this sword won't survive the carbon pressure if it gets wet!' Jambalee blurted.

She gasped in shock and horror fearing for James and his safety, continuing she said, 'So are you suggesting he could be carbonised?' She glanced around at young Tom, who now was positioned on the graceful Unicorn, and then she quickly flicked her gaze back to the teenager James, for whom she had once had strong feelings for. Frowning to herself she shouted, 'Jambalee, what are you doing? Are you sure about this?'

Halaconia was clearly rifled by how they had progressed and by the unknown dangers which lay ahead. 'Do you not realise the dangers of how dangerous Xle-Ha is?' Halaconia bawled.

On hearing and seeing a clearly worried Halaconia, both boys looked pitiful and scared.

James then turned to Halaconia. 'Halaconia, I don't know who this Xle-Ha is. It's like…the light of the world, a city on a hill cannot be hidden. We are going to be fine. We just have to believe. – Right?' James then gave a steely stare and walked off to his Unicorn.

There was a solemn silence; Tom was astounded. He glared at Halaconia for reassurance. Just as quickly, James then took hold of his beloved Unicorn. Again he peered intently into its gazelle-shaped eyes as he stroked his white, silky, drooping mane.

The light slowly faded away again, first turning into a shadowy grey, then becoming a sudden pitch black. A labyrinth had been created. Eventually only a few broken star lights were visible through the ruptured sky.

'Quick! Go back go to that crater, go…quickly!' Jambalee shouted. He gave a steely gaze, and with a fearful stare he glared at the two young boys and the luminous Unicorn.

The Calm beneath the Surface

Halaconia turned to face Tom. 'Tom, I must tell you—' She frowned, dropping her eyes. She then hastily grabbed his arm. 'Just be aware not to disturb the deep magma, that's the important explosive!' She was pensive and gazed at both Tom and James. Still frowning and very upset she continued, 'The eruption that you two are looking for is beneath the calm of that surface—that's where it is! I just have to let you know about the deep smog and ash below that surface. It will rise into the atmosphere and force itself out like a nuclear bomb.'

She hesitated to finish her sentence, and with a deep, nervous energy she gasped, taking in a deep gulp of air so as to not upset Tom. She then erupted back into her talk with the boys. '...Sharp and abrasive opaque devastation—it really is devastation for our galaxy. And Xle-Ha will be angry!'

With her waterlogged gazelle eyes, she turned to James. 'You are the light of the world.' There was a pause, and James placed his arm around Halaconia, comforting as best as he could. 'Darkness dominates our world, James. You must stay safe.'

James held Halaconia by her small hand. He gazed into her gazelle eyes as he sat her down on a rock. He stared at her face and said awkwardly, 'I'll be careful. I have the tools with me to help.' Then he bashfully smiled, waving her the hoop with feathers to convince her, hoping she would smile, too.

'Halaconia is ehmm…Aspero is he—is he…the one you are going to marry?' James had to ask the question that he so longed to hear even though he knew there would be no future between him and Halaconia. He had to hear it for himself from her.

Halaconia gazed at James and let go of his hand quickly. She moved away from the rock and stood up onto her hoofed legs. She fluttered her silver wings whilst gazing at James awkwardly.

The Dream Catcher

She said, 'James, I could never leave Oblivionarna, the land of my birth – your mother was the princess of Oblivionarna, and King Cepheus saw that she would be protected from Morkann. James locked by her honesty silently continued to listen, '...and Aspero is the one I will marry.' Halaconia slowly dipped her eyes and then averting James's gaze turned her back quickly just as Tom walked over towards James. There was a cold pause leaving James totally speechless. Not knowing what conversation was being discussed Tom blurted, 'Halaconia, we are going to try and cross that river.'

James gave a wiry smile to Halaconia, as she stared up into cosmic grey sky peering at the meteors wheeling through the space, hinting for a break in the sky for the rotating, green planet to show its face.

James leapt up from the ground and grabbed Halaconia's hand. 'You okay?' he whispered.

She nodded, averting her eyes. Tom glanced at James and then quickly back at Halaconia realising that something had happened and was said that he was not aware of.

Halaconia then pointed to the silver river basin. 'There it is. 'Carina's Drift'. The calm beneath the surface is in there. You will have to go in there - somehow.' She was firm in her sentence, and then she let out a deep sigh of air and flew high into the cosmic surround.

Tom turned quickly. 'Halaconia, where are you going?' he asked desperately.

'I will be back to help later.' There was an uneasy pause before she fluttered away quickly again into the airspace. She turned sharply to face James. 'When the red sun seeps through the golden cosmic stars, I will be back. Just remember not to trust any shadow after dark.'

The Calm beneath the Surface

James gazed in awe and nodded as she flew high into the distance, eventually disappearing. 'Wow!' he murmured to himself.

'Now what?' Tom said, trying to ascertain what James was so in awe of.

'Her!' James snapped, referring to Halaconia. 'That creature. She is just, something…I never know how to deal with her! He was perplexed and felt he wanted to say so much more than he could, even to Tom. James took in a deep sigh and then decided to concentrate on their quest to cross the silver river basin of Carina's Drift.

Turning to Tom, James checked his pocket for the Dream Catcher. 'Tom, take the magic powder out of your pocket. I think we are going to have to use it!'

'Sure,' replied an anxious Tom.

Chapter V
Carina's Drift

The boys trudged wearily on past the dark, dreary, bamboo-coloured vines which were entwined with brown, old lichen draping and falling uncontrollably through the dense, luscious, damp, water-soaked terrain. James ran on quickly ahead as the branches whipped past his head. He felt dizzy and nauseous as it felt they had sped through time across the terrain to the banks of Carina's Drift.

James stopped at the silver water's edge and glanced back at Tom as they separated and became two again.

'Tom, hurry up!' James shouted.

'I'm sure this is where we can get into the Drift',' James suggested as he began to intensely scan the terrain leading onto

The Dream Catcher

the silver liquid known as Carina's Drift. As he glared he could see a slight flame rippling through the liquid. It seemed to appear like soft fire was lurking beneath its surface. It was as if a soft glow of orange had kissed the silver liquid.

'Look at that!' James pointed excitedly, amazed at his finding. When both boys stared into the liquid, Tom turned to James and James turned to Tom.

'Where's the calm then?' asked an ever-inquisitive Tom as he looked fiercely into the deep.

James took hold of Tom's sword from the jewelled hilt and glided it cautiously through the silver liquid. He glared at the peach-coloured ripples it would cause. Both Tom and James were now able to see clearly the orange flicker of what appeared to be vibrant flames beneath the liquid.

'Did you see that?' asked James.

Tom was leading the Unicorn by his mane. 'Yeah. What was it?'

'I think that ripple of dark light is Xle-Ha!' answered a panic-stricken James.

'Gosh, is there no other way to get over to the other side?' queried Tom.

As the two boys puzzled over how to cross this dangerous river, James could see in the corner of his eye a broken meteorite. James had a sudden brain wave. He paced quickly to Tom and began to explain how he would capture the broken meteorite and throw it high into the sky so that it would fall. If James could do this, then it would allow the meteorites to be heated incandescence by the friction of the air, subsequently catching fire.

This process would of course then imitate the two boys crossing the river allowing Xle-Ha to show his wrath and be able to annihilate the meteorites and not the boys!

Carina's Drift

Tom listened intently to James and then glanced at the orange glow of this liquid. 'James, you know. Look at it!' Tom shouted. James walked closer and stared into the river.

'Do you see your reflection?' asked Tom.

'No!' James snapped defiantly. He gawped quickly into the strange liquid, which lay before him and then leaped up, astounded at the absence of reflection. Still in horror of no reflection he glared deep into the orange glow.

'What the—' he said with a puzzled look on his face. James knew that this opaque liquid was not just any ordinary substance for there was no reflection and the liquid seemed too still.

James turned to Tom. 'Tom, you know in chemistry, what liquid is it that catches flames?'

'Errh, I think it's…eth…ethanol!' Tom quipped, as he sniffed the heavy stench of alcohol spilling out from Carina's' Drift. Tom shrugged his hands at James, smiling smugly after all; he was the one with the scientific brains. 'So, how are we going to cross that - now?' he said frustrated at the silver liquid and smell.

'I'm not sure come on'. Replied James anxiously.

As both boys and the Unicorn, being led by James, walked carefully around the edge of silver liquid, the Unicorn suddenly jolted and jumped up terrifying Tom.

'Woh, what happened?'

James struggled to calm his Unicorn when the liquid, now known as ethanol, exploded breaking, slowly cracking open to display a strange, dark, fearful character.

He was covered with bizarre black markings on his face and muscular torso; his arms were powerful yet seemed to replicate a panther's limb. His hand was thick heavy, and paw-like, with nails sharp and pointed representing a deathly claw. His face was sharp

The Dream Catcher

and jagged with black markings tattooed across his face as if he were a tribal Red Indian. He had on his thick mop of black hair a skull of what looked like the open jaw of a lion or panther displaying its teeth in a toothsome grin. It was totally frightening, and both boys suddenly felt nauseous, petrified for their lives.

Tom stared at Xle-Ha's torso and at the distinctive markings, which were thick and black and danced on his torso rippling on each of his ribs covered in a toned flesh in an obscure design. Tom noticed that one of his arms was muscular and were covered with tribal black markings. However, the other arm appeared strong as iron and was draped with a panthers hide covering his flesh and the hand was sheltered by its claw ready for a kill.

"Wow—who is that?' nervously blurted James to Tom.

His eyes now wide-eyed in terror, Tom glared back at the strange character that had risen out of the ethanol liquid. As both boys were transfixed by the strange display, they could see the orange surface breaking, and as it did so a flame flickered.

Then Xle-Ha raised his arm and as he did so, a fire suddenly erupted in a wild whirlpool sporadically appearing until the whole of Carina's Drift was alight. The Drift was bright and fierce with orange and topaz red-yellow fire flames fuming out of the strange liquid and around all this heat was the calm and collected Xle-Ha!

James screamed, 'Tom, quick. We have got to get out of here!'

Tom ran and grabbed the Unicorn, which was buckling and nervously kicking into the air.

'Tom, come on. Just push him towards you!' James shouted, as Tom tried to control the creature. James ran to help Tom get hold of the Unicorn in the sweltering fervour.

The heat was intense and becoming hotter. The bright flames soared and danced like a tribal awakening. The sweat trickled

Carina's Drift

down James's face as he manoeuvred the Unicorn into the correct direction to get him out of the way from the flames from within Carina's Drift which now surrounded Xle-Ha.

'How does he just stand there, in those burning flames like that? questioned an agitated Tom.

'Come, on, let's just get the Unicorn and get out of here!' James moaned, struggling to control the unicorn at his discomfort.

The heat was becoming more intense and seemed as if it were burning the air. The sky had not turned black but red from the colours of the flames. As both James and Tom looked at Xle-Ha they could see that the abhorrent creature was smirking with a malevolent grin to himself and that there was malice in his features. The black thick lines on his body helped to promote malice unknown to the boys, but they were trapped in a liquid of ethanol, inviting them to put their arms into the fire flames below.

'Hey, Tom, what colour is this sky now?' asked James, as he frantically peered into the cosmic fume-filled atmosphere. 'Do you think Halaconia will come back?'

'I...I think she may, you know—' There was a pause and James took in a deep sigh and gave a steely stare to Tom. 'She did say, "When the sky turns red, I will come back!"'

The boys quickly settled behind a large half-broken boulder. Suddenly there was a swishing, gentle noise, and Tom sneaked his glance into the crimson air and could see Halaconia and Aspero gliding like Chinese lanterns towards them. She was accompanied by a large orange beast of some sort, but Tom and James were unable to make out the exact type of creature it was. They could also see Jambalee gliding beside her in the seeping comets floating through the sky. It was very difficult to see all of them clearly until they landed near the boys.

The Dream Catcher

Once Tom had seen Jambalee he felt assured that everything was going to be okay and that James would surely be able to rescue his princess.

Halaconia appeared along with Aspero and an large, orange phoenix Centaur; however, when all three had landed, it transformed miraculously into a giant fierce Centaur. His feathers on his head stood proud like a peacock tail all fanned out displaying its bright fireball colours of red, orange, and yellow.

Yet its strong, muscular, toned body resembled that of an ox—strong, fearless, and proud. Halaconia walked over to Tom and held his hand.

Then Aspero walked over to James and placed his strong, powerful hand on his shoulder. 'James, you have been chosen. We have been able to hold back Morkann and her army of Ghouls but Xle-Ha can only be defeated by YOU! We cannot take you further as my powers only extend to this edge.' Aspero dipped his head as he spoke.

As soon as Aspero had said the last word, everyone including James jumped back and glared at the fire burning. In the middle of the raging orange flames stood a strong, toned, muscular figure with his face painted with strange black ink in warrior-type markings, and his arms were draped in what appeared to be a black panther's skin including the claws which draped over his hands. His head displayed a firework of bright feathers all balancing carefully on the skull of a panther with its jaws wide open displaying its toothsome teeth. It was an evil sight.

James gulped and shook his head. 'That, fire—you want me to in there alone? Are you crazy!' James stammered. He glanced at each one of his friends.

Tom bit his lip and with a tearful glare interrupted, 'James, remember the CALM! Which means it is hot on the surface but it is probably freezing below there.'

James just nodded. Jambalee walked over to James.

'My brave one, take this.' Jambalee gave James his Shield of Life and asked him to hold it.

'We will be here for you,' Jambalee said, dipping his eyelids. There was a slight pause before Jambalee continued trying to reassure James of his strength.

James gave a steely stare. He was totally apprehensive about even attempting to go near the ethanol liquid burning furiously.

The flames were vibrant, and Xle-Ha glared through them like a poised statue. He was waiting—it seemed as though he were waiting for James. James gave a forlorn stare to Tom, Jambalee, and Aspero who were now all lined up watching and trying to guide him into the liquid.

'James, we are here. We will not let anything happen to you. You must have faith!' Aspero said.

James worriedly gazed back at his brother one more time who was holding and stroking the Unicorn. He paced closer as Xle-Ha gave a menacing stare through the flames at James.

James paced carefully, peering side to side as he cautiously took each step forward towards the blazing flames. As he approached the liquid burning he could the feel the intensity of its heat. He raised his arm to protect his eyes. The heat was sweltering. It was too hot; it burned and raged its anger onto his body.

James squeezed his eyes tightly shut, fearful for he could feel his sweat trickling down his forehead drop by drop. He then quickly turned away from the burning blue-orange fire flames, all the time trying to protect himself from these incandescence flares;

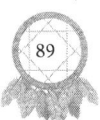

The Dream Catcher

still turning his back, he was able to make out the silhouette of Tom now in the shady distance mouthing to go forward and to continue his pace, using his hands as gestures asking him to use the magic hoop.

James could just about make out that Tom was now holding his hands together with his fists tightly clasped as if he were praying.

James had cleverly swung the Shield of Life over his back, so that it did not touch the liquid. James slowly closed his eyes as he cautiously took the crucial final step that would drop him into the liquid—the liquid of Carina's Drift. James stretched open his jaw with deep relief, and after a brief moment let out a gulp of awaited air. He breathed deeply and then dropped into the ridge and then slowly into the liquid. He paused and looked all around him, and through the burning, intense, orange flames which crackled as the sparks jolted yellow and blue fireworks, he could feel his legs submerging into the silver thick liquid.

At that very second Xle-Ha smirked, snarling at the brave James as he raised his arms which were covered in black panther fur skin. He roared violently, tilting his head back and displaying the old, wild, feline teeth from the panther's skull, which was pivoting precariously and decoratively on Xle-Ha's own head.

The skull of the black panther sat proudly like a crown on Xle-Ha's head between the spirals of brightly coloured feathers protruding pompously out of each side of his head. He wore it so elaborately whilst stretching out his torso and flexing his strong muscles like a peacock in search for its mate. This was the warning signal.

His elaborate charcoal markings of a forgotten Chippewa tribe etched all over his body worked hard to intensify the green, luminous, wild, mad eyes together with the open jaw which threw out the menacing razor-sharp fangs still stained with blood—all there to scare anyone who would dare tamper with the wild Xle-Ha!

James watched the great Xle-Ha in awe. He flinched nervously, blinking only twice whilst taking in some air.

Xle-Ha's hand, still draped in the claw of a raging panther, extended out to the burning flames trying to grab at them. James gasped, dropping his jaw wide open. He was now standing arrogantly in the liquid, and yet he could feel the heat generated by the flames roaring ferociously around him. It felt somewhat strange how the fire fumes were blazing viciously in a deep, inferno plume of vibrant colour yet beneath the deep, where James had now dropped legs into—it felt cold, ice-cold.

James glared with his waterlogged eyes, wide-eyed and fixated on the strange character he was now in view of. Then just like a shape-shifter, Xle-Ha elevated out of the liquid in a swirling red plume of smoke. He pivoted into the galaxy, and as he did so the flames became weaker and slowly fizzled out.

In a strange, swirling, revolving rage of purple smoke, Xle-Ha bellowed again loudly, 'I want the Dream Catcher. You have what is mine! Your dream will never be! Give it to me!' Xle-Ha raised his arms, engulfed in rage whilst snatching at the flames.

Xle-Ha, seething with anger, gawped intently. His eyes were burning red in colour, and with his temper he had clenched his fur-covered fist high into the remaining orange flames as if he were trying to catch them. He roared the roar of thousands of lions. So piercing was his wrath, that the Unicorn, waiting on the edge with the others, jolted and leaped into the air, shaking his neck and exulting in whatever it was that Unicorns exult.

Tom and Jambalee grabbed onto the Unicorn, tying to calm him, and Aspero held on to Halaconia. Tom, still holding the

The Dream Catcher

Unicorn with the others, moved closer towards James but did not enter Carina's Drift. Seeing James had dropped into the liquid, Tom shouted, 'James! Be careful! Hold up the Dream Catcher. He wants it. Give it to him!'

James scaled the terrain and then plodded steadily deeper into the liquid nervously as he kept his eyes on Xle-Ha's glare. James knew the hoop he held possessed some magic or had some significant meaning—that was why Xle-Ha wanted it.

'You must give me the Dream Catcher!' Xle-Ha roared furiously. The panther skull which sat proudly on his head tipped over his forehead and hence the panther's jaw dropped open to reveal the collection of razor-sharp blades shaped for a kill. The strangest thing was that it looked so real and not like a dead creature—so much so that it appeared as if it were about to leap out at James for a kill.

Both Aspero and Jambalee had now swiftly walked over to the edge of Carina's Drift and had joined Tom. They all gazed at him in amazement, waiting for him to say something.

James in shock and completely speechless had now frozen as he held on tightly to the Dream Catcher. He did not believe he would have the courage to step into Carina's Drift, which was now roaring and raging with orange and yellow fiery flames burning brightly within it.

Jambalee gave a warm smile, first at Aspero who was now holding Halaconia by the hand, and then quickly at James.

James peered at Aspero and then quickly scaled back at Carina's Drift. It was still alight, burning brightly, shimmering with all its light, yet Xle-Ha, still clad in his Native-American attire with panther hide covering his arms, stood angrily and proudly within it.

Carina's Drift

'James, you are brave and honest. This is why Xle-Ha had to leave, but I know he has not gone for long, and he will be back for the Dream Catcher that you have! I know now that he knows you have it, he will want it for sure, and he will be back with a vengeance!'

Aspero then nervously scaled the Sahara-like desert of sand dunes in search of the enemy Morkann. There were sporadic tufts of trees, acacia and baobab, and on-again off-again grasses and shrubs as far as the eye could see atop the brown earthen crust, a surface that looked as hard as stone and somehow even less inviting.

Jambalee interrupted, frowning cautiously at the young, strong, brave James.

'That tool you carry, James, is the tool of the Chippewa. The Dream Catcher is the tool which the Chippewa use. They created it, James. You know it is part of what you know as Dreams—the dreams which do not come true and to those dreams in which you pray and hope they will come true—dreams, James.' Jambalee finished with a deep sigh.

James listened intently as Jambalee began to speak as he stomped through the now-warm liquid, watching the blaze begin to fizzle out.

'This is what I was afraid of...' Jambalee hesitated, glancing at the strong James as the gush of cold wind slapped his face. 'You see that?'

James felt uneasy with the blast of wind that sporadically smacked his face. He turned to the others in desperate search for an answer. James dragged himself through the heavy liquid which displayed a shattered mosaic of a thousand reflections appearing as broken mirrors.

'Don't look at the reflection, James!' Tom squealed, trying to help his brother as he gazed in horror. But James was completely oblivious

The Dream Catcher

to everything around him; all he wanted to do was to get out of the menacing valley. James pulled himself in towards the edge where his graceful beloved Unicorn stood. The light was becoming dim, and his sight became poor, and yet the Unicorn stood proud like a dog waiting for his master to return. James peered at Jambalee, and then glanced back at Halaconia and then at Tom who was busy with Aspero.

'You have to tell me, what is so important about this thing that I carry?' James asked inquisitively whilst pulling himself out of the warm sludgy liquid.

Aspero gazed intently at the river as it transformed like a slithering snake to see the coiling of its burly currents, snatching at the shimmering of silver waves as it tried to grab the stars like scales in its mouth in a thick sulphurous stream.

Aspero's eyes narrowed. He glanced casually at James who stood still in shock and complete bewilderment as the flames slowly began to fizzle away.

'Which type of liquid burns in water, James?' asked an inquisitive and puzzled Tom.

'Ethanol! Tom, you know—C_2H_5OH. That's the science part! Tom, ethanol—smell it. In other words toxic alcohol! Can you smell it?'

James frowned angrily, sarcastically bellowing and goading Tom to move closer in order to get a good smell of the strange liquid.

Chapter VI
Beneath the Calm

'James what the—man, this is completely strong stuff!' Tom said with a turned-up lip. James moaned as he grimaced at the stench of the abhorrent smell.

'James, this smells like some sort of wine or something!' said Tom as he gently dipped his palm into the warm substance whilst stroking the liquid, causing heavy ripples of gloom to fade across the silver substance. As the ripples swam across Carina's Drift, Tom witnessed short, sharp flakes of broken mirrors wafting around, and as he peered closer he suddenly felt an ice prism flash and jump out at him with sudden spiky and jagged corners, each one displaying a shattered image of his mother, James, and himself.

'What the—wow, did you see that?' Tom exclaimed, jumping up in excitement as he watched the ripples die away into hundreds of broken mirrors of his childhood.

'Yeah, I did,' James answered slowly with a forlorn gaze. Both boys then looked at Jambalee and Aspero for their reassurance. There was a slight pause and then ever so carefully Jambalee gave a quick short nod, almost to assure the boys that everything was going to be okay. James steered back over to his unicorn and then

The Dream Catcher

grabbed onto his four-legged friend and walked over onto the other side of basin.

He watched intently as the liquid trickled over a fallen meteor and then dripped into an open, wide tributary; James peered deep into the clear as the shimmer began to break into thousands of silver crystals, each dazzling shards of the broken mirror.

'Look! Look! Did you see that?' James followed his reflection transforming into the dazzling shards of mirrors he was not to look into, and then as quickly as he blinked it faded away.

Halaconia gave a steely stare to Aspero and Jambalee before she flew over to them. Hovering, she said in a toneless voice, 'I will help you find her, James.'

James looked up at Halaconia and smiled adoringly at the strange creature for he knew she was going to help him reach his goal.

'You must walk this way,' beckoned Halaconia as she tried to guide both boys across the current until they were at the dry creek bed. The boys and unicorn staggered on, trudging in the deep, grey-soaked terrain, their footprints causing deep, sunken wells to appear. They followed the ridge down toward a patch of grass which was not green but was a shade of electric blue. The atmosphere, however, was engulfed in a soft, fresh, green mist that swirled and hovered around. Tom turned wide-eyed to see Jambalee and Aspero who were now lagging behind but were still in pursuit of the boys.

It had been some time and there was no sign of stopping. The boys were now beginning to feel tired, and their limbs were aching with a dull droning pain. The journey was becoming arduous and felt very long. As the soft, apple green cloud mist lifted, the dull patches of fiery crimson gradually glowed far beyond the cliffs of the mountains of the moon. Tom nudged James to gaze up into the

Beneath the Calm

horizon and to gaze at the thrusting spires of naked rock into the rugged old cliffs.

James slowly lifted his head, and as he did so, bright light stars shone straight back into his eyes, blinding him intently. Jambalee rushed over to aid James. He leant over to him, and whilst holding his head, placed into his mouth several drops of the powder from the magic pot which miraculously transformed into a thick medicinal liquid. After a short while James smiled, and a golden white light appeared brightly on the horizon, spanning out into a fan of a multitude of incandescent shades of swirling whiteness.

James's sleek, white, graceful unicorn trotted over and seemed to smile at him. It was really quite something surreal as James gazed in gratitude at his new family around him. First he gazed on Halaconia, then Aspero, so strong and powerful, and then he turned to Tom holding his Unicorn. For that split second James squeezed his eyes tightly and let out a call for his mother, Linda.

'Mum,' he hollered, as a single tear trickled from his sore eyes onto his torso.

In doing so, his call reverberated around the horizon. This caused a concerto of harmonic sounds bouncing off the mountainous rocks around, jumping from one crater to another.

'We are nearly here,' said Jambalee. 'You will find your dream very soon. You are a good person, James. I know your dream.' Jambalee gave James a stretched smile of assurance.

James sighed heavily. 'You don't understand— I don't know what it is. Right now, all I want to do is find that girl and to go home!'

Jambalee, smiling, placed his small yet strong hand onto his shoulders, and with a loving grin turned to face him. 'James, I cannot take you further as my powers only extend to this edge.

The Dream Catcher

You will travel with your Unicorn. You will carry the Dream Catcher sword and the Shield I gave you. That is all you will need from here.'

James gave a steely stare to Jambalee and took in a deep sigh, licking his lips.

Tom glared at his brother who now stood alone on the creek of the other side of valley. James looked strange—nervous and apprehensive about his journey alone in a land which seemed to be riddled with malice.

Jambalee gazed at James and bellowed, 'James, remember everything is good if your heart is good. You will succeed!'

James acknowledged his words and turned his back, very slowly pulling his Unicorn in line to walk on.

Chapter VII
The Lost Princess

James wondered on through the desolate plains of an unknown land past the protruding, jagged, razor-sharp spires of the Mountains of the Moon that stretched high into the galaxy where he was told a great Oracle sat on a craggy summit littered with spiky frost-shattered rocks angled like ancient tombstones.

He glared around at the drooping brown lichen falling from the green mountains and then swiftly back at the gleaming bleached rock with its deep, emerald water and blue foaming tears with the endless sky above; James was in awe at such a magnificent place.

At that moment he decided to bring some water to his Unicorn. 'Here, I'll get some for you. You thirsty?' he asked whilst peering over to the beautiful clear water. James lovingly spoke to his four-legged friend. He stroked his head and long slender neck and then trotted off to the green pond.

He walked towards the edge to bring some liquid to his Unicorn. He took hold of his shield and tried to balance some of the liquid onto it when he heard a melodious voice.

It was note, a singing note. He quickly jumped up and turned around. His heart was beating fast, pounding, running too fast to let his blood flow. Then he could see as clear as a crystal through

The Dream Catcher

the tropical waters tightly packed, black, basalt columns sticking out of the sea. The polygonal pillars were strangely regular, almost as if they had been formed by a human hand—or the hand of a giant.

James ran quickly over to his Unicorn and gave him some of the water and then directed him to the columns. 'She's there. I know she is. Come on.' James gently guided his Unicorn towards the caved rocks which fell over the basalt columns. It was part of the same ancient lava flow, which fell from the crater eruptions and after hearing the strange echoes from Morkann and her Ghouls they would cause the water to slosh around the cave, forming a rib cage of basalt columns.

James walked on, guiding his Unicorn, and then he rushed on not thinking of anyone. As he approached a massive, precariously balanced, broken slab, he was forced to glare up into the dark sky, and in doing so he could see that Morkann and her Ghouls had reappeared. They wailed and hissed around him, jostling him. James was frightened but then he remembered the Dream Catcher in his pocket.

He pulled it out inconspicuously, frightened as a mouse yet brave and strong as a lion. He succeeded, and he held it high into the air. He watched wide-eyed, his chest heaving as he took in deep slow breaths.

Morkann swished over to him, slicing the air with her long, grey cloak. 'You—you will not rule!' she roared her anger. Rage was etched on her beetle-laden face.

James dare not flinch; he just held the Dream Catcher tighter and tighter in his hand. He felt his face became red, and his knuckles were sore and were starting to ache. Then ever so slowly the web on the Dream Catcher began to glisten and dazzle in the starlight. The

The Lost Princess

brown beads started to turn clockwise then they turned the other way and transformed into a deep red colour. The feathers grew and became bigger.

James, amazed in terror, still held on tightly to the Dream Catcher as the sound of Morkann and her Ghouls intensified and became piercing. They wailed, hissed, and moaned. As they did so the Unicorn tried to protect his master, James, by nuzzling him. James felt stronger.

Morkann glided over to him and snarled at him, jeering with her evil, menacing panther eyes, she then turned to call her menacing Ghouls, to retreat.

After a short time the Ghouls began to die away and drifted into a deep labyrinth.

When all was quiet and James was sure that there was no one left around, the Unicorn first looked up at James with his big, blue, sapphire eyes.

It was now all quiet.

'Do you think they have all gone?' James asked his Unicorn even though it was not going to speak back to him.

James then gave a sigh of relief and ever so slowly dropped his arms to place the Dream Catcher hoop into his pocket. James patted his unicorn and peered intently at the Dream Catcher.

Shrugging his shoulders, he glared into the horizon, thinking deeply about the events that had just occurred. Then he scanned the vast surroundings. There he could see a massive, precariously balanced slab which was wobbling at a strange angle. James slowly trotted on further into the slushy marsh, and beneath the jutting black stone ledge, he could just make out a silhouette. He became anxious. Could it be the princess he was in search of?

The Dream Catcher

There she sat, hunched into a ball, knees tight against her chest, her damp clothes about her. He knew it, he was now sure. She was the person he had been searching for.

James rushed over and gawked for a good few seconds. As his eyes were unfocused he blinked slowly at the girl curled up in a ball. He wasn't sure on what to say.

'You—" There was a pause. 'It was you.'

She appeared surreal and ethereal and completely beautiful—something of a masterpiece. The girl looked up at him, and she was as beautiful as he had remembered, her dusky golden skin and her soft raven hair with her puppy dog, apple eyes begging to be saved.

'Yes, it is me. Princess Anna-Lisa. James, why did you come back?' she questioned, yet her longing was just as powerful as James's.

James was now on cloud nine. He had found whom he was in search of. Yet he was puzzled at her. She seemed so cold, distant. James walked over to her and held out his arm to lift her out from the ball shape she had fallen into. 'Come on. Let's go and sit here. I just wanted to see you and take you home with me.'

She suddenly opened her tear-logged eyes, glaring straight into his. 'Take me home!' she yelled in shock.

James was still totally unaware of the dilemma that had fallen before him.

'What do you mean?' James asked in deep shock.

'James, I am Princess Anna-Lisa, Morkann's step-sister. Did you know that?' There was a pause, before a steely James gazed at the princess, still soaked in her dreary, grey, tattered clothes. I can never be friends with my enemy,' she said sternly. As her voice began to quaver, she stopped suddenly and dipped her tear-logged eyes.

The Lost Princess

She spoke softly but in a humble manner, and although she stammered to complete each word the princess turned her back on a dazzled and bewildered James.

After a space of ten snails, James took out the Dream Catcher from his pocket and glared at it, holding it tightly, wanting it to do something, anything. He glared starry-eyed as the web again began to shimmer, and his thoughts then started to dart around his mind in a mixed-up muddle. He frowned and took in a deep gulp of air. Still holding the hoop, he watched it dazzle and gleam as he approached the princess.

'So that's it? You are just going to give up then, hunh?' James was feeling hurt, yet he felt some sort of connection with this strange creature.

She was now shedding droplets of tears from her soft, green-apple eyes but did not make any other faces. However, James knew she felt something for him and was being held back, but did feared Morkann's wrath.

'Why are you doing this to yourself?' He questioned her, but before she could answer, he blurted, 'I was told that if something is right and good then it was always right to do whatever I had to do.'

He grabbed her by her thin arms, pulling her closer to him. 'Look at me!' James insisted powerfully.

She was too fragile, too unsure; her heart raced as fast as a leopard with panting breath. She could feel every blood cell rushing through her veins. She felt anxious. They peered deep into each other's eyes for as long they were able to without blinking. He locked his stare into hers and just as quickly she averted his gaze, dipping her soft eyes to the ground bashfully. There was no noise, only the beating of hearts and the innocuous sound of strange shooting stars breaking as they fell. He was nervous, his hands were clammy,

The Dream Catcher

and he was breathing deeply. He lent forward and reached over to kiss her, but he suddenly stopped. It seemed too sudden—too quick. His blood quickened through his veins, and his heart raced quicker than a hare. After a short while, he nervously stretched out to take her hand. Her hand was thin and gaunt, almost child-like. He started to play with her fingers. There were no words uttered.

He watched her movement, subserviently giving his hand like a puppet. She slowly sunk her face into his chest, closing her eyes. James stroked her silky, luscious, burnished bronze hair as they then embraced. She closed her eyes and wished a thousand wishes before their lips locked into a soft kiss.

The Dream Catcher had worked, even if it were for that moment only. For that moment they were together. Perhaps it was the conundrum of emotions whizzing around inside James's head. The light shone brightly around them, and even the Unicorn again dazzled its horn. Something felt so right, yet it was so wrong for Princess Anna-Lisa even to smile let alone to love her enemy.

'Come-on lets go', taking her hand. James gently lead her to a path near a fallen crater.

'I know Morkann will have you killed, she will do anything to anyone, but we have to try and forgive and pray for her- do you know what that is?' James said smirking.

'But I tell you who hear me: Love your enemies, do good to those who hate you'. This is what is written, where I come from, and it says to 'love thy enemy and pray for those who persecute you.'

'How can you pray for someone like Morkann?' There was a pause as Princess Anna-Lisa pondered to herself about James. I like you–Prince of Oblivionarna; you are wise beyond your years'.

James glanced around at the dark basalt rocks surrounding him, wondering how he would get back home.

The Lost Princess

As they slowly trudged on through the dense terrain James then remembered his Mother, and the battle, which took place with Morkann. How she wailed about her being the true Queen, such wrath was shown that night. But then James also knew that very moment his Mother Linda, was the real Queen and that Morkann was envious of all. She would do anything at any cost even if meant she would have to kill her own step-sister Princess Anna-Lisa to gain control of the galaxy.

'You do know Morkann will have me killed, if she is to hear of this union?' Princess Anna-Lisa trembled as she spoke. James Peered down at the princess smiling, 'I know - but I am the Prince of Oblivionarna, you do know that, and that is going to make even more angry?.' James had acknowledged for the first time that he was a prince—a real prince. Perhaps this was his destiny?.

There was pause, and a cold, sharp wind slapped James across his face. A hundred bad memories danced around in his head. He was in turmoil with his emotions, yet he knew she had to be rescued. He had to take her home. He knew he had said something which he had stored in his mind. He let go of the princess's arms and pushed her slightly away.

'Maybe our lands will unite if they see us together,' James stammered nervously at his suggestion.

The Unicorn began to jump up, kicking his legs high into air. James could hear sluggish footsteps becoming closer and louder. He became nervous. Suddenly a crazily tilted path fell away from him, and he began a slow descent into a dark chasm. He had to let go of Princess Anna Lisa. A strange irrational panic caused him to descend without hesitation, and with a deep brow he warned Princess Anna-Lisa, shouting, 'Look out! Take the Unicorn! - Take him!'

The Dream Catcher

She frowned in anguish, nodding, and then turned to face the Unicorn.

At that very moment, Hakeem appeared with Jambalee, Aspero with Halaconia, and Tom. Tom ran towards his brother excitedly and relieved that he was well. James, in shock, gawked at the towering Hakeem as Hakeem roared, 'You, James have found the calm beneath the surface. It is written that you must be rewarded. Come, you must now go home. It is time.' His voice echoed around the tor, reverberating off the craters and meteorites scattered across the galactic airspace. There was a pause that felt like a lifetime, and at that very moment, James and Tom realised they were about to go home.

Reviews

Hi, just read the book extract:
Thought it was great, action packed and keeps you wanting to read on. The mythology references add an educational twist to the novel. Fantastic read!

Hope u have a good day.
Michelle xx
Sent from my iPhone
Michelle Beresford-Smart

Dear Rayner Tapia

I am writing to thank you for the amazing book you gave me. It is a fantastic book and I would want to read more. This book makes my heart beat extremely fast and it is non-stop action from start to finish. Thank you so much for the book.

From James Richards aged 12

Dear Rayner Tapia,

I would like to say I really enjoyed 'The Dream Catcher' because of it's action. I found it a very imaginative. ~~[scribbled out]~~
The best bit was when James and Tom were in a battle with the Ghouls. It was tense and dramatic.
Thankyou for giving me your book.

        Love from
          Arjun Thind.
            Age 13

A Note from the Author

Dear Reader,

The Dream Catcher is book three of five books in a series that will endeavour to take your imagination to another dimension.

I have created a world where truth is always sought and yet, just like on earth it is sometimes difficult to locate. The characters I have created, will entice you and invite you into their realm and indeed into their planet.

I really hope you all enjoy reading this short novel. Please leave your comments on my website:- www.theadventuresoftommcguire.com

God Bless you.